STEPHANIE DOYLE

The Doctor's Deadly Affair

ROMANTIC

SUSPENSE

For Bobby, Mary Grace and Kev-Kev,
On the cusp of your future…
Good luck.

SILHOUETTE BOOKS

Recycling programs
for this product may
not exist in your area.

ISBN-13: 978-0-373-27720-9

THE DOCTOR'S DEADLY AFFAIR

Copyright © 2011 by Stephanie Doyle

Visit Silhouette Books at www.eHarlequin.com

Printed in U.S.A.

"How did they die, Wyatt?"

Murder. The word was foreign to Camille. Almost surreal. But three people were dead and she knew that she wasn't responsible. Someone else was.

"That's what the medical examiner has to find out," said Wyatt. "But how hard could it have been? Three people, completely vulnerable after surgery. Nurses, techs, any hospital staff really could have come and gone. A pillow to the face. A fifty c.c. syringe of air into the IV. I don't know."

"I can't believe this is happening." Nothing had ever prepared her for this. There was no rule for defending herself against a murderer.

Wyatt advanced on her, his face close to hers. She could feel his intensity and in some ways, it frightened her. "Well, you need to start believing it. It is happening. Your eyes, your ears need to be open at all times. You need to be watching everything and everyone coming near you.

"Because I'm fairly certain that the next person this killer wants dead…is you."

★ ★ ★

FEB 2 5 2011   ROMANCE

Dear Reader,

What's your worst fear? I'll tell you the truth, mine is snakes. Petrified of them. Big ones, small ones, deadly ones—for obvious reasons—harmless ones. It doesn't matter. Show me a picture of a snake and I'll cower in the corner.

For me a heroine like Camille Lawson makes perfect sense. She has all these fears. Some rational—after all, someone is out to kill her—and some not so rational. Such as car-door handles, public utensils and strange refrigerators.

The thing is, what scares us isn't always something we can control. I wanted to explore that idea in this book and what it takes to overcome those fears. Love helps. Camille finds that out along the way in *The Doctor's Deadly Affair*.

Hope you enjoy this story!

Stephanie Doyle

P.S. I love to hear from readers and can be found on Facebook or my website www.stephaniedoyle.net.

Books by Stephanie Doyle

Silhouette Romantic Suspense

Silhouette Romantic Suspense
Undiscovered Hero #792
Suspect Lover #1554
The Doctor's Deadly Affair #1650

Silhouette Bombshell
Calculated Risk #36
The Contestant #52
Possessed #116

STEPHANIE DOYLE,

a dedicated romance reader, began to pen her own romantic adventures at age sixteen. She began submitting to Harlequin at age eighteen and by twenty-six, her first book was published. Fifteen years later, she still loves what she does as each book is a new adventure. She lives in South Jersey with her cat, Lex, and her two kittens who have taken over everything. When she isn't thinking about escaping to the beach, she's working on her next story idea.

Dear Reader,

Yes, it's true. We're changing our name! After over twenty-five years of being part of Harlequin Enterprises, Silhouette Books will officially seal the merger by taking the company's name.

So if you notice a few changes on the covers starting April 2011—Silhouette Special Edition becoming Harlequin Special Edition, Silhouette Desire becoming Harlequin Desire and Silhouette Romantic Suspense becoming Harlequin Romantic Suspense—don't be concerned.

We'll continue to have the same fantastic authors, wonderful stories, eye-catching covers and emotional, compelling reads. We're just going to be moving under the overall company name, which will make us even easier for you to see in the stores, on the internet, and wherever you usually find us!

So look for the new logo, but remember, beneath the image will be the same promise of romantic stories of love, passion, adventure, family and a whole lot more. Just the way you like them!

Sincerely,

The Editors at Harlequin Books

Chapter 1

Camille Lawson swung open the door to the establishment and stepped inside. He was where the nurses at the hospital said he would be. Sitting at a small table, his drink halfway to his lips as he read the newspaper. For a second she watched him without him noticing her. Tall, lean, ridiculously handsome with ink-black hair that had a smattering of white at the temples.

The white hair should have made him look old. Instead it made him look dashing.

She wondered again if this was the stupidest idea she'd ever had, but she'd come this far.

Approaching the table, she set her briefcase on the chair opposite him as an announcement of her presence.

"Hello, Wyatt."

At first he looked surprised to see her. His expression quickly changed to smug. "Camille. What brings you to a place like this? I thought you disdained addicts."

"I do." She sniffed, then assessed what he was drinking. "I see you haven't kicked the habit."

"No intention to kick it. I like it too much."

"I don't have to tell you, enough of that will kill you."

"Nope." He took a deep gulp—to annoy her she knew.

"I have a business matter I would like to address with you."

One eyebrow crooked. "This," he said with a deliberate pause, "should be interesting." He waved to the chair across from him in invitation and folded up his paper.

She shifted her briefcase to the floor and sat cautiously. It wasn't beyond him to do something silly such as kick the chair out from under her. Had they met when they were children, she had no doubt he would have taken pleasure in putting gum in her hair and giving her noogies.

He'd been that kind of boy. She was sure of it.

Taking a sterile wipe from her handbag she wiped the tabletop in front of her. It wasn't her habit to come to public drinking or eating establishments. They were infested with germs. On half washed glasses and utensils. On tables where people rested their hands and elbows. Even the smell of the place, which announced its purpose as soon as a person stepped through the door, made her queasy.

How many thirsty, needy people had passed through here today alone? How many of their individual germs had soaked into the fabrics and settled on the leather surfaces?

So many people. All of them carelessly touching everything around them…with their hands.

She suppressed a shudder.

Having done all she could do with the surface, she put the wipe in an empty Ziploc bag, which she carried for such an occasion, and made a mental note to keep her hands in her lap as much as possible. She would have preferred to sit on a stool with no arms and less chance of contamination, but she didn't imagine he would be bothered enough to move to a different location.

At least not for her.

Reaching for the files inside her case, she started with her pitch. "It's probably nothing. I don't even know why I'm here but—"

"Oh, no." He held his hand up to stop her. "If you came here to discuss business with me, we do it on my terms. You'll need a drink."

"You know I don't enjoy—"

"For me. For whatever it is you need from me," he corrected. "In the spirit of colleagues."

This was so typical of him. Doing anything he could to push her buttons. There was no *spirit of colleagues*. Not between them. Not after... She shook the painful memory from her head. For now, she needed him.

"Fine," she said through gritted teeth.

Wyatt held up a single finger and a girl in a green apron bustled over. "Can I get you something?"

In a fit of bravado Camille raised her chin. "I'll have what he's having."

"Nice," he murmured.

The waitress, who apparently knew his order, didn't bother to confirm what he was drinking.

"Can we get down to the matter at hand?"

He took another deep gulp. "Go for it."

Camille withdrew a folder and handed it to him. It was the case review of her last patient. "Donald Morose. A sixty-one-year-old man with multiple blockages. Three weeks ago I opened him up and did a quadruple bypass. He was recovering, on schedule, then died."

"Okay," Wyatt said slowly.

Camille pulled another folder. "Samuel Ross, a fifty-two-year-old man, also with multiple blockages. He needed a triple bypass. Once again the operation was successful and he also was recovering on schedule."

Wyatt flipped open the folder. "Until he died."

"Correct."

"Camille, what do you want from me?"

This was the tough part. "I want you to tell me why they died."

He barked out a laugh but she could tell he wasn't amused. "I resigned from my position as God a few months back. I'm afraid I can't help you."

Camille struggled to hold on to her patience. "Those surgeries were perfect. Those men were recovering. There were no complications. They should not have died."

Wyatt shook his head. "Camille, people die every day. For Pete's sake, you're a doctor. You know that. It happens."

"Not to me. Not when I know I executed flawlessly. I have over a ninety-seven percent success rate in bypass surgeries. To have two patients not recover in the span of twenty-seven days is statistically improbable."

"Are you serious?"

She could hear the incredulity in his voice. And she knew what she was saying could sound unreasonable. But she also knew the medical history of those two men to the minutest detail. She knew what the odds of survival were on both. She knew how she had performed and she knew what their post-op status meant. They were recovering. They were getting better. Donald had been one day away from discharge. They shouldn't have died. Which led to only one conclusion.

One impossible conclusion.

She had missed something.

"Really, Camille? You think you are that much in control? You think *this* is going to kill me," he said, raising his drink. "Your convoluted notion that you have ultimate power over your universe is going to kill you."

"Look, I don't want a lecture. I want you to review the files and tell me if you think I missed something. Some common denominator. Something that might have caused these two patients to die."

"Something other than having their chests cut open and arteries bypassed you mean."

"Yes. Something other than that."

"You said these men died post-op?"

"Yes."

"Then there would have to have been a review."

Camille nodded. "There was. The medical examiner found nothing obvious and concluded both men died as a result of complications after surgery. Most likely an embolism."

He closed the folder and leaned back in his chair, arms crossed.

Here it came. She knew he wouldn't do this for nothing. She knew there was going to be some condition. She braced herself for many things.

Her parking spot. Never going to happen.

A tour of duty in his outpatient clinic where she was sure to catch every virus floating around this season.

An embarrassing public announcement. Something along the lines of her agreeing he was the greatest doctor she had ever known. This, of course, would be a lie. She'd worked under Schlossberg, who developed groundbreaking techniques in organ retrieval. He was, without question, the greatest doctor she had ever known.

After her grandfather, of course. All doctors paled in comparison to her grandfather. Should she be forced to say otherwise, she would need to do it with her fingers crossed.

"Say it," she prompted, ready to hear the worst. "What do you want?"

"First, I would like you to drink what you ordered."

The waitress put a large mug in front of Camille. It was foaming.

"Grande, triple-shot, mocha with whip cream and extra foam."

"Thanks, Christy." Wyatt, because he was Wyatt, paid the waitress at the table, probably including a ridiculous tip rather than standing at the counter with everyone else in the coffee shop. Christy was happy to indulge him.

"No problem, Doc. See you tomorrow."

Camille flinched as she studied the mug, determining the best way to attack. She took another wipe from her purse and scrubbed the edge where her mouth would touch. She would have preferred to clean the mug herself, but this would have to do. She dumped the wipe with the earlier one and braced herself.

If she came down with the plague, it was going to be his fault.

"You know you're a child," she said as she took a sip of the über-caffeinated, sickly-sweet drink. Of course it was delicious but that wasn't the point. "All this caffeine and sugar are not good for you. A poor diet can lead to a weaker immune system which could lead to—"

"A cold. Yes, I'm aware of the ramifications, Camille. Now for my next request."

"Wait," she said. She took another sip of the coffee only because she figured she'd damned herself already by taking the first. "Before I agree to what I'm sure will be an absurd demand, I want to make certain we understand each other. I want only the best medical opinion. I don't want any tricks. None of your silliness. No woo-woo medicine."

He scowled. "Forget for a minute you're a grown woman using the word *woo-woo*. I will reiterate for the one thousandth time, using non-Western medicine to diagnose and treat patients is not *silliness*, Camille. It's sensible and it works."

"I heard the nurses talking the other day. They said you brought in a psychic to read a patient's health aura."

Wyatt shrugged. "I had trouble determining what my patient's problem was. I had met the psychic at a holistic conference in Tahoe a few months back. I gave it a shot."

"Said psychic being tall, blond, buxom and gorgeous."

He smiled like a wolf. "Ooh, is that jealousy I hear in your voice?"

"Certainly not." Mostly not.

"The woman—her name is Drusilla by the way—"

"Of course it is."

"—actually concluded what I had already begun to suspect."

"That the patient had a symptomatic aura?"

"That the patient was faking it. The aura was perfectly healthy. When confronted by the psychic the patient no longer felt that he could lie. He concluded that Drusilla, unlike a standard medical doctor, had detected the truth. Can't very well have a dishonest aura. He broke down and I was able to steer the patient toward psychotherapy. I believe he's making a recovery."

"You say all this as if it was a success. You perpetrated a fraud."

"I did no such thing. I treated a patient—correctly I might add. That's what I'm in the business of doing."

Recognizing that they were once again heading down a path that would lead to shouting, cursing and foot stomping—mostly by her—Camille backed off. "Fine. You have different methods. I accept that."

"No you don't. That's our problem."

"We don't have a *problem*." Saying it the way he did implied they had a relationship with a problem in it. That was not the case. "I'm only asking that for this case review you don't employ any…nonstandard diagnostic techniques."

"Got it. No *woo-woo*."

All right. The word did sound ridiculous.

He flipped through the files again, briefly skimming. "Can I speak with the families?"

Camille sighed. She'd hoped he wouldn't have to. She had a very unrealistic wish that he'd find something simply by looking at the case reports. But if cause of death was that simple, she would have found it herself. And if she hadn't, then the medical examiner would have.

"Both families are distraught. Of course. So if you have to speak to them, do so as delicately as possible. I would appreciate that."

"Plus you don't want to raise any alarms. No sense in stirring up trouble and having the families file a malpractice suit."

Her hand slammed down on the folder, causing him to jump. "I'm not doing this to cover my ass. I'm not doing this because I think I did anything wrong. I'm doing this because I know, damn it, that those men should not have died. Not by my hand. And I want the answer as to why they did."

The smile was back. "I love it when you go all hellcat on me."

"Will you do it?" she asked, ignoring his taunt.

"I will. For one teeny-weeny thing."

"Name it." Camille braced herself again for the request.

Mochas for a year. Clean his office at the hospital for a week wearing a costume of his choosing…so not going to happen.

"I want a second date."

Of all the things he could have asked for that was the one she didn't see coming.

Chapter 2

Camille headed to the top floor of the hospital where the administration people had their offices.

Ruby, the hospital CEO's senior assistant, was sitting at her desk staring at the computer screen. The young girl was competent if a little oblivious at times. She had an addiction to tanning beds that wasn't at all flattering with her red hair.

Camille cleared her throat.

"Oh. Hi, Dr. Larson. I'm sorry. I was reading this article on the swine flu epidemic. Scary stuff."

Camille wished the assistant hadn't said anything. She had a hard enough time coping with the germs that covered so many of the surfaces in the hospital, she didn't want to imagine what types of illnesses they led to.

One mental health condition was surely enough for a person. No need to add hypochondria to her neurosis list.

Spermatophobia, the accurate term for germaphobia as

Wyatt referred to it, was difficult to live with. And given the snicker value of the name, it wasn't something she walked around discussing with most people. As a scientist, a doctor, she reasoned that her obsession for cleanliness and fear of dirt and germs stemmed from latent childhood insecurities she had yet to overcome.

She also knew it made her weird. Which she hated. Only there was nothing to be done about that.

"Hi, Ruby. Is Delia available?"

"She's not in a meeting or on the phone. But be prepared. The grant committee meeting is looming and she's flipping out about it."

Camille thanked Ruby for the heads-up then knocked on the executive's door before entering.

Delia Marsh sat behind a desk covered in paper, looking the way she always did: harried. Her colored hair was showing roots that had been neglected. Any lipstick she'd started the day with had already been chewed off. And the buttons on her blouse were off by one, if the crookedness at the collar was any indication.

The chaos of Delia was always startling to Camille. But she understood why. Delia never used to look like a woman on the verge of a nervous breakdown. No, it was Camille who had done that to her.

Ten years ago Physicians' Memorial Hospital had been a small facility with a solid reputation. Situated in the suburbs of New Jersey across the bridge from Philadelphia, it didn't try to compete with the hospitals in Philly.

Camille had chosen it as her place of practice for exactly that reason. She didn't want to have to deal with doctors' egos. She didn't want to have to jostle for position among the staff. She wanted to do the work.

In the years she'd been doing that here, the hospital had gone from small and solid to one of the most renowned hospitals for thoracic surgery and heart transplant on the East Coast. Camille Larson was a hot commodity, making Delia infinitely busier. Running a hospital, in many ways, was like running a company, and reputation was everything. Due to Camille's success, it was like growing from a Mom-and-Pop shop to a Fortune 500 in the course of only a few years. With that came more pressure and responsibility than Delia could sometimes handle.

Of course, Camille wasn't only to blame for the hospital's success. Wyatt had helped establish the hospital's reputation before she arrived, before he abandoned surgery and focused on diagnostics.

And there had been Dr. Logan Dade.

Dade was everything Camille despised in a doctor. Arrogant, with a God complex, the patients were the very least of his concern. All that mattered to him was the organ that beat inside the body. Good-looking, skilled and rich, the man was a walking cliché. But he'd been a damned fine surgeon.

Not quite as sought-after as she was, though.

Camille liked to pretend he'd left Memorial to work at City General because he wanted a bigger stage. But the truth was this stage hadn't been big enough for the both of them. At least for him and his ego.

Delia, having almost adjusted to the demands of running what was now a big hospital, and trying to expand it even more, hadn't been pleased by Dade's departure. In fact, she'd been downright surly about it for the past month.

It wasn't a rational thought, but Camille was almost certain Delia blamed her.

Not that she would voice her opinion. After all, without Camille the hospital had nothing.

"Yes, yes. Come in, come in."

Camille obeyed and stepped into the maelstrom. Beyond

the papers scattered over the desk, there was a credenza behind her that bore the spillover. Then there was the floor which Camille was fairly certain hadn't been carpeted with paper.

"I know," Delia said catching Camille's stunned expression. "But I had yet another assistant quit...."

"You don't pay them enough."

"I don't get paid enough," Delia retorted. "Anyway, things are a mess. I've got the people from the Heart Health Foundation coming in at the end of the month and if I don't have everything ready for them, I might have to jump off the roof."

"Please don't."

Delia looked at her as though she was crazy. Oh, she thought, that was hyperbole on Delia's part. Camille never did well understanding or expressing humor.

"Anyway, everything has to be in order. This is it. The big one. If we can get that grant money, we'll finally have enough to add that new wing we spoke about. State-of-the-art technology, brand-new and all yours. Sound good?"

Camille didn't need much more than an operating room and scalpel to do her work, but she knew Delia was excited by the prospect of expanding the hospital.

"You said those foundations are more reluctant to give grants to smaller hospitals."

"They are. They assume we're all about delivering babies and handing out bandages, but you changed that. This paperwork is to prove how we are getting it done with smoke and mirrors. This is the chance of a lifetime. Everything I've been working toward..."

Delia trailed off and Camille could see that, for a moment, she was completely overwhelmed. Lost in thought over the potential for success or failure. Camille wasn't sure which.

"I'm sure it will all work out."

Delia met her gaze and Camille could see that she was not pleased by her words. Delia opened her mouth to say something. Something that wasn't going to be pleasant but she stopped herself and ran her hand through her hair instead. "What do you want?"

"I wanted to let you know I'm having Wy— Dr. Holladay review my last two fatalities."

"Why? You told the medical examiner and me nothing went wrong in those surgeries."

"Nothing did. That's why I want Dr. Holladay to review. I don't know why those men died."

"Because they had bad hearts. There was an autopsy, there was a conclusion. Drop it."

"I can't."

"Jesus, Camille, you can't save everyone."

No, but she had saved both those patients. Until they died. "He's going to take another look. You know how he is…sometimes he sees what others miss."

Delia pulled her hand through her hair again, coming away with strands that she had to shake off her fingers. "Is he going to contact the families? Because we've heard nothing from them. If I get a call from a lawyer because of his poking around and making them think you did something wrong, so help me, Camille, I don't care how good you are, I will come down on you like a ton of bricks."

"He will be discreet. And I didn't do anything wrong. I need a better explanation for why two patients in recovery suddenly died."

"Fine. Let him look. But if he finds nothing, then it ends. You understand?"

"I do."

Delia's eyes stayed focused on her. "I don't need to be

worried about you, do I? Maybe some time with Dr. Rosen might help."

Dr. Rosen was a psychiatrist on staff who often helped with grief counseling for families.

Camille definitely didn't need time with him. She'd done the counseling route with him a few years ago to treat her condition. It had proved ineffective. Mostly because she didn't believe in the science as a whole any more than she believed that a person could read another person's aura. Talking about her issues didn't translate to solving her problems. At least not in her mind.

Besides, Dr. Rosen liked to ask her questions she didn't want to answer. Often they were intrusive and annoying.

A pragmatist, Camille recognized that in many ways her thinking was restricted when it came to the edges of science. Unfortunately, she had no desire or urgency to expand her mind. She was locked in. It made her a perfect surgeon and a most fallible human being.

"What is Wyatt's plan?"

The question startled Camille. "Uh…I assume he'll review the case files, my notes. He'll do a general background medical history and if he contacts the family, it will simply be as a follow-up call. They shouldn't suspect anything."

"Because there is nothing to suspect, right?" Delia's voice rose to a dangerously high octave. "I'm serious, Camille. I can't have this right now. It's bad enough you had two patients die right before I'm about to go before the Foundation asking for money for a new damn heart wing. If you know of anything that might have caused—"

"I don't. This is for my curiosity."

"Your curiosity," Delia said, clearly disgusted. "I hope that helps you sleep at night. Because if you jeopardize this—"

"I know. A ton of bricks."

"And then some. It's bad enough you pushed Logan out of here, I can't have you thinking you run this place now because of that."

There it was. The source of Delia's recent behavior toward Camille. She'd known it on some level, she just hadn't wanted to accept it. She should have felt better now that the truth was out, but she didn't. Dr. Logan Dade had made her life hell for a brief time while he was here, and it seemed he was going to be responsible for more trouble now that he was gone.

"You think I made him leave."

Delia tensed. "And if I do?"

"Then you would be wrong."

"Look, I know he was an ass who couldn't handle second place behind you, but still. Two amazing heart surgeons are better than one when asking for money for a new wing. His leaving was bad timing. I—I needed him. If you only could have respected him more."

"Respected him? You mean placated him, don't you? Pretend I couldn't handle surgeries he could? Not take the lead role on transplant teams? Had sex with him? He claimed to want that as well. Maybe I should have given in."

Delia's lips pressed together.

Camille was satisfied she had the last word. "Exactly. I could have done none of those things, so his leaving was not my fault."

"Fine, fine. Just make sure you don't stir up any needless trouble now. I'm putting all my eggs in your basket. I'm counting on you. This hospital is counting on you."

Camille nodded. She turned and had made it to the door when Delia stopped her.

"So what does he want in exchange?"

Hand on the doorknob, Camille didn't turn around, certain the flush in her cheeks would give her away.

"Come on, give. I know Wyatt and he didn't agree to do a favor for you without asking for something in exchange. Is his ratty old Jeep going to be taking up space in the parking lot next to my Beemer?"

"Give up my parking space? Never."

With that Camille left quickly, shutting the door behind her before Delia could ask a follow-up question.

No, Camille wasn't going to have to give up her parking space. What Wyatt was asking for was much, much worse.

"Say *ahhhh*."

"Marcus, do as the doctor says."

The little boy in front of Wyatt pressed his lips together and shook his head authoritatively. Under no circumstances was he conceding. According to his mother, this was the second case of strep he'd had in a year and his pediatrician had been considering a tonsillectomy.

Wyatt wouldn't comment that he didn't necessarily see the correlation between the two, other than when the kid got strep his tonsils swelled and must be painful. But the fact that the strep was recurring…that was an issue.

The pediatrician, however, was now out of the picture since the mother had lost her health insurance. This had brought her and her son to the health clinic at Memorial. The clinic wasn't free. But Wyatt did everything he could to make care affordable. This visit would cost the woman forty dollars.

The antibiotics—the ones she'd probably been skimping on, giving her son maybe half the prescribed amount until he felt better in order to save money—was where the clinic would kick in.

A knock on the door had Wyatt turning on his swivel seat. He was hoping for a nurse who would have ideas about how to get a kid to open his mouth.

What he got was a masked invader.

Shaking his head at Camille's somewhat dramatic entrance, he tried not to smile as he faced the boy.

"Come on, Marcus. You can do this. All you have to do is open your mouth."

"Dr. Holladay."

He could hear the impatience in her voice through the white surgical mask she wore.

"In a second, Camille. I'm with a patient." Wyatt jerked his chin over his shoulder. "See that crazy lady behind me with the mask. You don't want to be like her, do you? Never showing your mouth to anyone."

The boy looked over Wyatt's shoulder and studied Camille standing there with her arms crossed over her chest, her eyes narrowed and the rest of her face covered.

The boy seemed undecided.

"No, you definitely don't want to be like her. She's a scaredy-cat. A germaphobe. You want to end up like that? Walking around with a mask over your face…for life?"

He could hear Camille huff behind her protection. "I believe sharing my medical condition with patients is a violation of the Private Health Information act."

"I'm not disclosing private health information if the conditions aren't real." Wyatt said to the kid, "One little word, Marcus. Otherwise I'm going to have to find you a white mask."

"Ahhhhh." Wyatt had the tongue depressor in the kid's mouth before he could blink. He easily saw the infection and did note that the tonsils were extremely swollen. "It looks like strep."

The boy's shoulders dropped as did his mother's.

"And the tonsils are really swollen."

This, he could see, alarmed the boy. The pediatrician must have used the word *surgery* or perhaps an even scarier word like *tonsillectomy* in the kid's presence. "There is only one course of treatment I can think of…ice cream."

"Ice cream?" the boy rasped.

"Lots and lots of ice cream. Maybe some milk shakes or sherbet thrown in to mix things up."

The kid's jaw dropped open, his eyes wide. "But I love ice cream."

"Then it's lucky for you that's the cure."

"This is ridiculous. Ice cream is not the cure for strep throat," Camille chimed in.

"Don't listen to her, Marcus. Who trusts anyone in a mask like that? Can you do me a favor? Wait out in the hall by the reception desk and I'm going to talk to your mom. I've got to let her know what flavors work best."

"I like vanilla the best, but I'll even eat strawberry if I have to. It's got fruit in it."

Wyatt patted him on the shoulder. "Good man."

The kid left and Wyatt swiveled to the mother.

"I know what you're going to say," she said. "But I don't have… I mean, I brought him here, but a prescription for antibiotics…even generic…is going to be a lot and I don't have—"

She stopped herself and Wyatt's heart broke. As it did every time a patient came in and had to decide between their health and the rent, or their children's health and food for that month.

"Mrs. Langdon, the clinic will help you out with the prescription. We use a discount pharmacy and can work out a payment plan that can bring the cost down to a couple of dollars a week."

The relief in her was palpable.

"But here is the thing. You need to finish the entire prescription. You can't stop giving him the meds when he feels better. By doing that you're not killing the strep, which is why it keeps recurring. And each time it does, the infection gets worse and the necessary antibiotics need to get stronger. You don't want that."

She nodded. "Last time he seemed fine and there was almost half a bottle left. Then he got sick again and I used the rest, but then that was gone and a few weeks later here I am."

"I understand. Promise me. The whole prescription. Don't stop until it's gone."

"Yes, Doctor."

"Okay, Margaret at the desk—who is probably giving your son a grape lollipop if I had to guess—will help you with the financial paperwork for the prescription." Wyatt scratched out the order and signed his name on the pad.

Illegibly. Because that's how the cool doctors rolled.

The mother took the script and with a watery smile left the treatment room.

Satisfied, Wyatt faced what he hoped was a woman impressed with his bedside manner. Especially because he planned to give her a large dose of his bedside manner in the very near future.

But he couldn't tell much behind the mask.

"Dr. Larson, what can I do for you? A mysterious ailment? An urgent need to see the doctor? I understand… take off your clothes and I'll see what I can do for you."

"You're a child."

"I don't think so. If I were, I wouldn't necessarily want to see you with your clothes off."

She stamped her foot a little bit and he felt the corresponding hit to his heart.

She was nuts. Filled with insecurities and control issues.

More often than not she was condescending to his practice. Her sense of humor on her best day was nonexistent. Except, for whatever reason, he found her hysterically funny.

She was nothing his first wife had been and nothing he ever imagined for himself in the future. He preferred blondes for one and her hair was un-enhanced brown. Long, she forever wore it back and clipped up. He never understood why women who had long hair chose to wear it tucked away. Beyond that, Wyatt liked women with a big smile and an easy attitude to match his own, and Camille Larson was as buttoned-up as a woman could be.

He couldn't remember the last time she smiled. Maybe that's why she wore the mask.

"I want to know if you've made any progress with the case reports."

"I have not. Haven't even looked at them."

Her eyes, which were a normal hazel—nothing to write home about—glared at him.

"Don't give me that look," he told her. "We had a deal. You go out with me then I'll review the cases. First one. Then the other."

"Are you serious? You're waiting until our date?"

"It's sort of how this favor process works. If I review the cases, then you might decide to renege." In fact, he was sure she would. She wouldn't do anything so dishonest as to flat out tell him she had no intention of holding up her end of the bargain. However, she would have no problem delaying and putting him off indefinitely with some flimsy excuse like an emergency surgery.

"I don't believe you. This is a matter of life and death."

"Not life, just death. The cases aren't going anywhere and we had a deal. You go out with me and the very next day I will review the cases."

She looked away from him and he could tell she was trying to formulate her next argument. Her foot tapped on the linoleum to the beat of her brain. He didn't see her thinking. He heard it.

But nothing she could come up with was going to deter him. Because, for whatever reason, the prickly, uptight, unfunny hypochondriac, with the brown hair and hazel eyes, made his heart beat and his stomach flutter and he wouldn't even mention what she did to all regions south.

"Why are you doing this to me?" she asked, her voice tight. "We tried this, remember? It was horrible. We argued. You were nasty."

"You threw a glass of water in my face."

"Because you were nasty."

"I wasn't nasty. I was honest. You were condescending."

"I wasn't condescending, I was…curious."

He had her cornered. "Then there is no problem with us trying it again. I wasn't really nasty. You weren't really condescending. If you avoid drenching me, it should be a lovely evening."

"Fine. But not this week." Her hand reached for her throat and he knew what was coming. "I feel something, possibly strep, coming on. If you could review the cases, and as soon as I'm feeling better—"

Wyatt barked out a laugh. "You don't have strep. You have an active imagination. And if I waited until you felt perfectly fine, we'd be dead before the date happened. It's now or never, Camille. I'll pick you up at your place tonight."

"Tonight!" she squeaked. "I can't possibly be ready by tonight. I don't know what I'm going to wear. I need a dress and shoes. And perfume…"

Her voice trailed off as he could see her running through

the categories of things women needed to have in order to go out on a date. What thrilled him was knowing that she wanted to look pretty for him. She wanted to smell good. She might disagree with him out loud, but deep down he knew she wanted this second chance almost as much as he did.

"Camille, whatever you wear I'll think you're lovely."

He could see vulnerability in her eyes and it touched him. She wasn't good at this. He knew that. This meant he had to be good enough at this for the both of them.

"Trust me."

"Okay," she whispered.

She turned to leave and he found he couldn't stop himself. "Oh, and Camille, remember to lose the mask."

Her hand rose to the white cotton that was still stretched over her mouth.

"I'm going to want to have access to those lips."

With that, she opened the door and, with everything she had, slammed it behind her.

Chapter 3

Wyatt made a right onto the street where Camille lived. He'd been surprised the first time he had picked her up for a date to learn that she preferred living in a small single-level ranch house rather than some sleek, sophisticated condo or town house. Being on call for Memorial meant she needed to be close, but Old City in Philadelphia wasn't much farther away than sleepy town suburbia.

The street was lined with big oak trees and the houses were dominated by families with young children and dogs if the crowds playing on the street were any indication. It was after seven o'clock but in late summer the sun was still up and a game of kickball was in progress.

Carefully, Wyatt negotiated around the kids of varying sizes and ages and approached Camille's house. His plan was to park on the street, but her street always seemed to be lined with cars as the driveways only accommodated one vehicle per family. He spotted a black car idling directly across from her house and figured he got lucky. Putting on his blinker he waited for the person to pull out.

After a moment, when the car made no move to leave, he assumed he'd been wrong. Maybe the person had parked. But as he was about to drive away the black car roared out in front of him, speeding down the street to the end of the block.

Jerkoff. Shaking his head, Wyatt maneuvered his Jeep into the vacant spot.

Once parked, he paused for a second before getting out. It was a thunderbolt to realize his hesitancy was based on nerves. Nervous for a date with Camille Larson. The idea was absurd, but there it was. This date was important and if he screwed it up…again, he didn't know how many other chances he would get. It wasn't like he could count on Camille to ask him for favors on a regular basis.

With one last glance in the rearview mirror he checked the knot in his tie and his teeth as a precaution. Yes, he'd showered, shaved—something he did only when the scruff on his face was about to turn into a bad beard—and put on a tie. An article of clothing he only wore when forced to attend either a wedding or a funeral.

That was one of the perks of working solely at the clinic in the hospital. Without the hassle of a practice, he could spend his days in scrubs rather than real clothes. It was like wearing pajamas. Hugh Hefner knew what the hell he was doing when it came to being comfortable all day.

But this was a date and a date called for a tie, didn't it?

Acting quickly, Wyatt pulled the silk from around his neck. He was being ridiculous. A tie would be over the top. Hell, if he was going to wear a tie, then he should have brought her flowers.

Flowers. Oh, shit.

He should have brought her flowers. They would have softened her. Or made her suspicious. It was hard to tell. Wyatt tossed off the sports coat and threw it into the back seat of his Jeep. He rolled up the cuffs of his button-down shirt and felt halfway normal again.

This was a big date, yes, but he needed to be himself. He needed to be comfortable. In truth, he was probably going to have to be comfortable for both of them, so shucking the tie and coat was dead on the right call.

Jogging up the front steps, he rang the bell and waited. Through the beveled glass panes on the side of the door, he could see movement. Fidgety movement. She was either straightening her hair or her dress. As soon as the door opened the nerves he thought he'd gotten control over flared up again, but he was less concerned with them now that he knew she was equally nervous.

There she was before him with her hair down around her shoulders, wearing a conservative black dress and low pumps. She smiled softly and one thought dominated his thinking.

He wanted her.

He'd worked at the same hospital with Camille for over ten years. She'd done her residency there and stayed on after it was finished. He'd allowed her to scrub in on his surgeries. He'd critiqued her technique. He'd taken breaks with her in the coffee room on the fourth floor surgical lounge.

But it wasn't until a year ago that he finally woke up and saw her. Saw all her complexity and wanted her.

"Did you want to come in? Or do we have reservations somewhere?" Her voice was soft but clipped in a way that told him she'd spent her whole life on the East Coast. A shame, because a few years of California living might have helped her unwind a bit.

"We've got time."

She seemed undecided so he moved forward until she had no choice but to back up. Once inside he took the time to study her fortress of solitude more closely. A workaholic, he might have expected sparse furnishings and the bare minimum.

Instead there was color. An explosion of color. A yellow couch. Green walls, a patterned rug over hardwood. A lounging chair with what looked to be an impossibly soft blue blanket tossed over it.

Not a surprise that her cat took residence on the comfy blanket.

"And what's his name again?"

"Her name. Aphrodite."

What the heck did that say about Camille? She'd named her cat after the goddess of love, beauty and sex. Yet she did everything in her power to conceal those very traits about herself.

Wyatt sat on the edge of the lounge chair, but the cat didn't budge. Instead she pushed her head under his hand as if demanding that he stroke her. So he did.

Camille stood with her hands clasped together awkwardly. "Can I get you something to drink?"

How long had it taken her to come up with that line? he wondered?

"Sure."

"I have wine. Red or white—" Her face fell and he could see the color leak from her cheeks. "Oh, I'm sorry. I forgot."

Wyatt shrugged. "It's okay. Sometimes I forget, too. I can't tell you how many times I've ordered a burger, fries and a cold beer only to realize that I can't have the beer."

"Is it hard?"

Sobriety wasn't easy. Wyatt could admit that. But after

five years it was definitely easier. "I'm used to it. And happier than I was as a drunk."

"I have club soda," she offered.

"If you have a lime, I'll worship at your feet forever."

She smiled a little and retreated to the kitchen that was on the other side of an arched opening from the living room. Wyatt took a look at the artwork on the walls. No prints of O'Keeffe and Monet for his girl. No, the artwork that dominated was the real thing. Oil on canvas. A fairy tale scene in a forest. A woman alone in a café. An explosion of muted colors that at the center contained a couple dancing.

Stone cold and practical, Camille Larson was at heart a romantic. He'd known it. When he'd finally woken up and saw her for who she was, he knew she had a big mushy heart that was buried in ice.

She brought a glass of wine for herself and handed him a tall glass with fizzy clear soda and a hearty chunk of lime. "So where are you taking me?"

"I've got a place in mind. But we've got time. Sit down and relax."

Camille chose the couch across from the lounge, her eyes falling to where Wyatt's fingers still played with Aphrodite's ears, he noticed.

She shook her head. "You know it occurs to me, now that you've…recovered…well, you could go back to surgery. You were a brilliant surgeon. I learned a great deal from watching you."

Wyatt smiled. "I have no intention of going back to surgery."

"Why? That doesn't make sense."

Not to a woman who valued surgical talent above all medicine. "Trying to lure me away from my woo-woo ways?"

"You need to stop using that word. I only meant that you had talent."

"Thank you. I had exceptional talent. But here's the trick. I had to stop being a surgeon because I was an alcoholic. But I was an alcoholic because I was a surgeon."

She shook her head as if rejecting such a premise. "Was it the pressure?"

"No, I thrived on the pressure. I loved it. It was the chest cutters." He shuddered with the memory of the feel of cutting through bone.

"If you didn't want to talk about it, you should have said so." She crossed her legs and folded her arms as if she'd been insulted. She thought he was making light of the situation but he wasn't. Still, he understood her pique. It wasn't a normal thing to say. Whoever heard of a surgeon who hated to cut open a body?

Wyatt leaned forward, elbows on knees, the club soda fizzing in the glass and making a lot of noise. "I never felt like I was worthy."

"We don't have to—"

"No." This was important.

He had blackmailed her into another date for many different reasons. The most eminent one being he wanted to get into her pants. Having been denied two months ago had left him in a constant state of sexual frustration. But he knew sex was a fleeting thing. If he'd wanted to, he could have found someone else's pants to get into without much of a hassle. If he'd really wanted to, he could have forgotten Camille completely.

But he didn't want to. He wanted to be with her. On this date with her. In bed with her. Which meant she was more than some person who he worked with who he happened to think was hot.

So he would tell her who he was and they would see what she thought…together.

"I had a very easy life, Camille. Great family, easy upbringing. Great grades, popular, an athlete. I became a surgeon because, other than being an astronaut, it was the most exciting thing I could think of to do."

She smiled. "It is."

The smile helped. It relaxed him. "It is. But all that time I was cutting into people and opening up their chests and holding their hearts and their lives in my hands, I thought I wasn't worthy. I didn't respect the job the way I should have. I didn't take it as seriously as I needed to. These people trusted me."

"And you saved them. Many times over."

"I did because I had nimble hands and a sharp mind. But it felt like luck. I didn't care about the breakthroughs, the new techniques, the new technology. Not until someone pointed it out to me. I didn't go looking to improve myself. I did what I had always done and relied on talent. And one day I took out the chest cutters and started cutting through the ribs of a woman on the table and I realized I shouldn't be doing this. The patient deserved someone who cared more. She deserved the person who treats the cutting open of people with reverence and awe. I wasn't that person."

She opened her mouth as if to reply, but he could see she didn't know how. She was one of those surgeons, he thought. He knew that about her. She didn't do a job— she lived her calling. It's what made her more than just a surgeon. It's what made her special.

"Anyway." He stood and set his glass on the coffee table. It was easier to pace during this part. "It started to eat at me. Day after day of cutting people open. I drank to ignore it. I drank to squelch it…but deep inside I think I drank because I knew it would get me out of it. It would destroy everything I had worked for and I was okay with that."

"I'm sorry."

He studied her face and wondered if that had done it. If his confession had ruined whatever chance they might have had. He wasn't proud of himself. But at the same time he knew his struggle with alcohol had defined him more than any other event in his life had.

"Don't be. I'm a better person today. I care more, I feel more, I explore everything more than I ever did before. I had lived, I am ashamed to say, a shallow existence. I took everything for granted. Now I don't."

"You make it sound like becoming an alcoholic was a good thing."

"No, I don't mean to say that. I could have done all this self-evaluation without the bottle. But a person who thinks he's the luckiest and happiest man alive doesn't really take the time to look at things too closely. The booze got me to the place I needed to go. I needed to be unhappy, I guess, and realize why I was unhappy, before I could fix myself. So it wasn't a good thing. It was *the* thing."

"Okay. I don't know if I totally understand."

He would have been shocked if she did. "You don't need to."

"But I accept that you don't want to return to surgery."

His lips twitched at her cool statement. It was on the tip of his tongue to tell her he didn't need her acceptance of his decision. But she wouldn't understand that what she said was condescending. In her mind she was stating a fact.

And he couldn't deny that it pleased him on some level, that she did accept him.

Uncomfortable with his scrutiny she fidgeted in her seat. "This is supposed to be a date and we've gotten so serious."

Good point. Normally he wouldn't have touched on the heavy stuff with any other woman, on any other second date. But once again, Camille made him behave differently. It was as though he needed her to accept him for everything he was. All his faults.

"I only said that about the surgery because I thought if you came back, Delia might not be so upset with me anymore for allegedly running off Dr. Dade. I know this is going to sound crazy, but she blames me for his departure. Today we sort of had it out."

Wyatt wasn't sure if that was the truth, but he was willing to play along. He'd spewed his soul on her open-toe shoes. He figured she needed a few minutes to recover from that.

"Ah, yes. Logan Dade. Memorial's finest cardiovascular surgeon until you finished your surgical residency and started to obtain more referrals from every cardiologist in a hundred-mile area. How devastated he was."

"Why do you sound happy about his devastation?"

"Because my opinion of Dr. Dade, in a word, is… asshole."

Camille's cheeks flushed but she giggled slightly behind her hand. Then her smile fell. "He used to ask me out. All the time."

Not a surprise. Dr. Dade pursued every eligible and non-eligible woman in the hospital. The size of his sexual appetite was superseded only by his ego. The rumors of his sexual exploits—mostly spread by him—were still legendary. Everyone had wanted him and he had wanted everybody in return. Except Camille.

"And you said no."

"Of course I did. For one, there were times when we were called upon to work as a team during a heart transplant. Any type of emotional issue could complicate a surgery like that and I wouldn't risk it. For the other, I could tell he…"

"What?"

She shrugged her shoulders. "I could tell he didn't really want me. Wasn't really attracted to me at all. He did it to…humor himself. To prove that he could have everyone if he asked. It's sort of how I felt when you first asked me out."

That hurt. To be put in the same category with Dade on anything was painful, but for her to think of him in those kinds of terms made him question if she knew him at all. "Why?"

"Because I'm not what you usually go for. I've been at Memorial almost ten years. I know all the stories about you. I knew your wife from the holiday parties."

"Ex-wife," he clarified, feeling no need to discuss the particulars of his marriage or divorce.

"I knew all the women you dated from the hospital after you two split. I'm nothing like any of them. They were all… tall and gorgeous and…lively. Fun. So when you asked me out I assumed you had…"

"Run out of people to date?" He tried to control the irritation in his voice.

"Something like that."

In that sense he couldn't blame her. She was right. She was nothing like anyone he'd ever dated before. His odd attraction might have made sense if she'd fed him a love potion. Only she didn't believe in love potions.

Which meant these feelings were based on something else. He was here, tonight, to find out what.

"Why did you say yes?"

It was a trick question. He knew why. He walked toward where she was still sitting on her sofa, her legs crossed at the ankles. The glass of wine, now empty, dangled from her fingers. He could see the flush on her cheeks deepen as he got closer. Could see her pupils dilate. As a physician and superb diagnostician he was trained to look for symptoms and add them up until they gave him the answer.

Camille averted her gaze. And when he took another step closer, she stood as if to head to the kitchen. To safety. He clasped his hand around her upper arm and squeezed gently. "Why?"

"I should put our glasses away. And we should be going. Even though it's Tuesday night, places will still be crowded."

"The place I had in mind won't be crowded. Trust me. Tell me, Camille. Why did you say yes when I asked you out when you thought I was no better than Dade?"

"I didn't say that," she corrected him. "I thought your reasons were similar, but I know you're not like him. You don't look at every woman as a conquest."

"Thank you for that at least. And you're right. A man at my age, with what I've gone through, I hardly feel the need to conquer anything. I asked you out because I wanted to get to know you. Why did you say yes?"

She stared at him and he could feel her uncertainty. She didn't want to believe him and that fascinated him. She was one of the most intelligent, driven and committed women he'd ever met. She was gifted in her talent but had the work ethic to back it up, which made her extraordinary at what she did. Yet here she was so doubtful of herself as a woman that it made him want to scream. Scream at every man who had ever overlooked her because the brain inside was so big.

"Because I…said yes. But it was awful the first time."

It was. The whole evening had been awkward. Conversation was difficult at first. When they finally found something to talk about, it was a topic on which they strongly disagreed. She was condescending, he became surly. When she finally pushed him too far, he snapped and called her a name. Like a ten-year-old he'd reverted to the oldest trick in the book. That's when she'd thrown the glass of water in his face.

He'd gone home that night thinking if he never spent five seconds in her company again he would be a blessed man. But when he woke up the next morning he was hard from dreaming about her and he knew that *they* were not done yet.

It was there. That magical *it* that could happen between two people who seemed all wrong for each other, but were drawn together like the moon to the earth. His plan was to bide his time, slowly start talking to her again. Keeping things easy and friendly.

Ha ha, what a horrible date that was...we should stick to coffee in the future. I'll make sure mine is iced so as not to cause any damage in case you douse me...ha ha.

Yeah, he had it all worked out. They could laugh about the date. He could discuss her cases. He would win her back one inch at a time, even if every day he suffered for the want of her.

All of those good intentions fled when she presented him with a golden opportunity to blackmail her. She needed his opinion and he needed her.

"It won't be this time," he promised as he moved in to place a simple kiss on her neck, just under her ear. He smelled perfume, which he knew she'd worn only for him.

"You'll get frustrated with me like you did before." A sigh caught in her throat.

He heard it. Knew what it meant.

"No, I won't. I'm prepared to be much—" he kissed the other side of her neck "—much more patient." His mouth dipped to the front of her throat to that tiny swell of soft skin. He could feel every quick breath with his tongue.

"So where are you taking me?"

"I'm taking you to the place I should have taken you the first time."

"The Cheesecake Factory?"

Wyatt smiled and in return she gulped, which meant she absolutely knew he had no intention of taking her to the Cheesecake Factory.

"No, Camille, I am taking you to bed."

Chapter 4

Camille dropped her wineglass on the carpet. "Oh, no."

"Leave it."

His arms were coming around her and she was falling into his hold. God, she was weak, but when it came to Wyatt Holladay she always felt helpless. The day she first saw him she knew she wanted him. It had been the strangest sensation, as it was really the first time she'd ever felt such instant sexual attraction. She'd had sex in her life. Mostly because she knew it was something people did and she'd gone through a phase in her life when she so wanted to be normal.

But seeing and wanting someone in a single moment had never happened to her before. Then she'd talked to him, all his easy charm and confident sexuality pouring out, and she knew he would never be hers. She wasn't the kind of woman who would attract him, and she wasn't the kind of woman who could convince herself that she was that kind of woman. She'd been almost relieved to find out he was married.

Because delusional Camille was not.

This, however, was no delusion. His mouth on her cheek, on her neck, was real. His arms lifting her off the floor, it was really happening.

"Bedroom."

"Down the hall." She couldn't believe that she got the words out. Couldn't believe that she was even considering letting this happen.

Let him have you for a little more, the woman inside her whispered.

Wyatt carried her down the hall and easily found her bedroom. It wasn't frilly, but it wasn't sparse either. A checkered white-and-blue duvet. Lots of big plump pillows. Her taste. Simple and soft.

Wyatt set her down on the bed and cupped her face. Immediately he went to work on the buttons of his shirt, revealing a tight white undershirt. She had no idea why it was so but seeing him in his undershirt was sexy as hell. Once his shirt was off, he pulled the undershirt off as well and what she had previously thought of as sexy did not compare to what she was seeing now.

His chest was covered with matted hair, some gray mixed in here and there, but the muscles were defined and begged to be touched. So she did. Reached out and touched him.

"Yes, that's it, baby. Touch all you want."

Since he insisted… But when she rose from the bed so she could put both hands on him, she felt him working the zipper of her plain black dress. In a wisp of time he had it open and the fabric was falling around her feet. Dressed in a white cotton bra and thong, all her vulnerability came back to her.

She couldn't do this. She wasn't the type of woman who could simply do this.

"I can't."

Wyatt used both hands to frame her face. He looked down at her body and then in her eyes and smiled. "Yes, you can."

"No, really. I can't do this. You should leave."

She could see disappointment in his face, but it was quickly followed by determination. "Do you want me?"

"I…that doesn't matter." Wanting him was as easy as drinking a glass of water. It was having him that she couldn't risk.

"It's the only thing that matters. Camille, do you want to make love with me? Right here, in this bed. That's all you have to think about. Not tomorrow. Not the day after that. Just us right now."

Us. The word was foreign to her. But then he was kissing her eyes and forcing them to close. He was nibbling on her ear and that felt good. Her arms were circling his back and it was as broad and strong as the rest of him.

He pulled away to give her a chance to answer. "You need to tell me yes. I'm not going to push you if you're not ready."

Did she want him? Yes. Did she want to make love with him now? Yes. Did she think she could have all that and still come out unscathed? Probably not.

In this moment, with him in her arms, she might be willing to risk it. She nodded and, for a reward, he kissed her mouth. A small quick kiss that didn't come close to satisfying her. But he was inching away and working at his belt. He undid the buckle, and dropped his pants, kicking off his shoes and socks in the process. He tossed the bundle of clothes on a chair near the door.

That was Aphrodite's chair. Camille wondered what she would think finding man-scented clothes on it.

Then he pushed his boxer briefs down over his hips and she couldn't think about anything at all. He was naked. She had a naked man in her bedroom for the first time in so long she didn't want to think about it. Suddenly, she wanted to do everything at once. She wanted to fall on her knees and take him in her mouth even though she'd never done anything like that before. She wanted to climb on top of him and ride him until she came. She wanted everything. But she did nothing. She was frozen in place.

Forcing herself to act, she reached for his erection. It was thick and hard and long and everything it should be. She shuddered with the idea of how this was going to feel inside her. She squeezed him and his head fell back as a soft groan emerged from his mouth. She wanted to hear that sound again so she pulled her hand up and then stroked him until he made it.

But then he was tugging her hand away. She was doing it wrong, she thought. Leave it to her to be the only woman on the planet who couldn't give a decent hand job.

"Too much," he said, moving close so he could kiss her neck. "I'm not going to make it. And I definitely want to make it."

She didn't understand but comprehension was always difficult when a man was nibbling on her ear.

"This first time is going to be fast, baby." He was edging down the straps of her simple bra. She opened her eyes to see him staring at her breasts as he slowly pulled away the cups. With his fingers he brushed along her nipples so that they hardened even more. He teased both with the lightest touches until she thought she was going to scream.

Pinch them! Please pinch them!

But the words would be shocking. Crude. It wasn't like

her to demand things in bed. It wasn't like her to even want things to be done to her.

He didn't pinch them. Instead, he lowered his head and sucked them into his mouth. And that was much better, she thought. He pulled and pulled her whole breast nearly in his mouth and she thought she might climax if he kept doing that, but he eased away.

The bra he'd manage to unfasten during the sucking fell to the floor, and he skimmed her panties over her hips. His hands playing with the cheeks of her bottom, rubbing them, seeming to delight in their round firmness.

She rode her bike a lot.

"Yes, this first time is going to be fast. But I promise the second time will be slower. More drawn out. The third time we can play with each other and the fourth time…"

Camille gulped and, in turn, Wyatt chuckled.

He picked her up and laid her out on the bed. She felt him lower over her and the sensation of the body-to-body contact almost made her climax again. She could feel his knees working between her legs, pushing them apart, forcing his reality on her.

"Are you on the pill?"

Camille tried to think about what he was saying, but she could feel his penis brushing along her sex, teasing her with his size and intent.

"Camille?"

"Yes," she said. "But you should… A condom… I don't have…"

"I do. But I don't want to use it."

Camille took her eyes away from his erection as it settled on her belly and instead looked at Wyatt.

"You know I'm checked regularly and I haven't been with anyone for a while. And I've never not used a condom but…"

"Then why?"

He shook his head and she could see he didn't know how to explain it. "I don't want to use one with you. I want to feel you and I want you to feel me. Nothing in between."

She nodded, which said everything about the trust she felt for him. Trust she didn't know she had for anyone. Immediately, he reached between their legs and she felt him push the head of his erection inside her.

She was wet, had been since he announced he was taking her to bed and everything in between had added to that. But he was big and the stretching feeling made her feel like a virgin again.

"Damn, you're tight," he moaned even as he pushed his way farther inside.

She couldn't tell if it bothered him or not. She wasn't any good at this. She never had been. Throwing her arm over her eyes, she turned her head to the side.

"Oh, no, you don't." Wyatt pulled her arm away and then interlocked his fingers with hers, holding both of her hands over her head. "Look at me, Camille."

She closed her eyes and shook her head. In retaliation he gave a short aborted thrust that drove him deeper than she thought she could handle, but felt better than anything she'd felt in so long.

"Look at me."

This time she obeyed and was rewarded with another thrust, this one more steady and even.

"That's it. I can tell it's been a while but it's like riding a bike."

"This is nothing like riding a bike."

Wyatt laughed. He released one of his hands and brought it under her bottom so he could lift her to him, bringing them even closer together. His chest rubbed against her sensitive nipples. He was buried deep inside her and his eyes wouldn't leave her face. He could see everything she was feeling. The pain of his fullness, the pleasure of it. She knew the pleasure embarrassed her more.

"Oh, babe," he groaned then leaned down to whisper in her ear. "I'm not going to be able to hold out. I promise, promise next time will be much slower, but you have to let me. You feel so damn good. I knew it would be like this. I knew it."

Letting him wasn't really an option. He had total control over her body and she was okay with that. She felt him pick up his speed, heard the harshness of his breath in her ear. She thought about whether she could orgasm. She didn't normally during intercourse, but he pushed down on her hips as he thrust inside and it hit her before she could finish the thought.

She was coming with a man inside her and it was the most intense experience.

He shouted and jerked between her legs and she quickly looked up to see his face tight with agonizing pleasure. He was beautiful.

In a huff, he collapsed against her. He turned his head toward her, and brought his hand up to force her head toward him. He kissed her then and let his tongue slip inside her mouth. She realized it was their first real kiss. He'd been inside her, made love to her, but now he was kissing her, slowly and deliciously. And this was almost as good as all the rest.

Finally he rolled away from her and she felt him slip out of her body. "Come on," he said moving off the bed and tugging her along. Once she was on her feet, she swayed a bit, but his arm around her waist steadied her. She wondered where they were going and why they had to be there so fast.

He started to pull down the covers of her bed. "We'll take a cat nap before we start again."

A cat nap. Aphrodite would appreciate that.

He stretched out in her soft and simple bed. He was hard and hairy and anything but simple. The contrast aroused her all over again. She slipped into the bed next to him and instantly he settled her against his chest, wrapping his arms around her.

"Sleep," he commanded.

There was no way she was going to sleep. It physically wasn't possible with so many thoughts racing through her mind.

What did this mean?

Why didn't he want to wear a condom?

What was going to happen when she saw him at the hospital?

Were they ever going to make it to dinner?

But even as the questions continued to roll through her mind, the heat of him behind her lulled her into closing her eyes.

She was asleep in seconds.

It was the feel of his lips on her neck that woke her. She was lying on her stomach and he was half on and half off her back, but he was kissing his way down her neck. Then his lips grazed over her spine and she tried to stay still.

Lower. Lower. He tongued the spot right where her back met her butt and there was no way she could control her slight shudder. Then with a playful slap on her bottom, he let her know he knew she was awake.

"Round two." His voice was gravelly and hard and it aroused her as much as his mouth did. He came over her fully, his legs between hers, his furred chest pressed against her back. He pushed his hands under her chest and cupped her breasts, lifting her enough that he could play with her nipples. Pinch them, make them hard until she arched her back and twisted her body, showing him without words what he was doing to her.

With heavy thighs, he pressed her legs apart and she gasped at the feeling of being opened this way. Then he pressed down on her and she felt the head of his sex enter her body. The sensation was extreme. She was on the bubble of all this anticipation and she wanted to scream with it.

Pushing her bottom up at him because she thought she needed to lift her hips for it to work all the way, she tried to tempt him into action. But instead of letting her, he used his weight to press her into the bed as he pushed himself fully inside her. The angle was different and the pressure was extreme. And she didn't know whether to laugh or cry or scream.

"Oh, that feels good." His voice grumbled above her.

Yes. Yes, it felt good. But when she opened her mouth to tell him, he pushed down again, thrusting deeper and she couldn't make a sound. Then he spread her legs a bit farther apart, her sex rubbing against her three-hundred-dollar Egyptian cotton sheets, as he set up a slow easy pace. Sliding in and out of her as though he was never going to stop.

It was delicious.

She must have whimpered or begged because he laughed evilly in her ear. "No mercy. I told you this time is going to be nice and slow."

Each word was punctuated with a thrust. One more and she found herself falling over the edge of bliss, moaning and twisting underneath him as her orgasm rushed through her.

Not that he seemed to care. He was relentless. He didn't

speed up, but he also didn't slow down. He just continued to pump inside her until she came again.

And again.

Round three took place in the shower. And it was everything he said it would be. He fell to his knees in front of her and did things with his mouth that were sinful. Then he let her run her soapy hands all over his body giving her all the leeway she wanted to enjoy his erection.

Slumped against the shower wall, the warm water rushing over her satisfied body, she concluded she wasn't going to live through the night. Camille also decided it was a very nice way to die.

"Come on, sex fiend. You need to eat."

He was standing in her bathroom, a towel wrapped around his hips. He looked relaxed and completely at home. Camille found herself focusing on the sight of his big bare feet on her pink bath mat.

"I figure we'll order in," he said as he ran his hand around his jaw as if debating whether he needed to shave. She knew he'd shaved for their date. His face had been cleaned of scruff when he arrived at her door and it made her happy that he'd taken the time to look nice for her. But his beard must grow rather quickly because she'd felt the scruff of his cheek on the inside of her thigh when he was doing the sinful thing with his mouth.

She didn't want him to shave very often.

"Pizza okay with you? Or what about Chinese?"

Camille shut off the shower and shook her head. Not to expel the water from her hair but in an attempt to gain some mental ground. Wyatt reached out his hand to help her from the shower stall. She took it even though she'd been getting out of this shower stall on her own perfectly fine for years.

Once she was on the bath mat with him, he pulled the towel off his hips and used it to dry her. Her shoulders and arms. Then her breasts and stomach, working his way down to her legs.

"You'll need to do your hair yourself. I don't know how to make those turban things."

"Turban things?"

"You know the way women wrap their hair up in the towel. I think it's hot by the way."

Camille bent over and wrapped her hair in the towel. When she looked at herself in the mirror she didn't think she looked particularly sexy. But Wyatt was gazing at her through the reflection and the wolflike smile was back. He ran his hands over her breasts and seeing him touch her made her shudder again.

It couldn't be possible, she thought. After so much sex she couldn't respond to him again.

"I know I said four rounds, but we need to eat first. I need energy." He kissed the side of her neck then left the bathroom.

"I say pizza. A large one with lots of meat on it," he called to her from her bedroom.

Camille found her robe on the hook inside the door and wrapped herself in it, closing the ends over her chest. She walked back to her bedroom to find him putting on his pants and T-shirt.

"Please tell me you like meat on your pizza. So many women don't and—"

"Get out."

She couldn't do this. She couldn't have this man in her house with his big bare feet and his wicked mouth. He'd made her be someone else for hours, but now she remembered who she was. She was Camille Larson. She was a brilliant surgeon. She was a solitary individual.

She didn't have great sex. She didn't shower with men. She didn't enjoy post-sex pizza.

"Camille."

She shook her head. "No, I mean it. I can't…" The panic was nearly overwhelming. "You need to leave."

He walked toward her slowly as if approaching a wild animal. "I know you're freaked out by this. I know this isn't typical for you—"

"How do you know anything about me? You don't know me. We went on one date. One horrible date. And this… this was just sex."

It wasn't anywhere close to *just* sex. Which was why she was about to have a panic attack. She really didn't want him to witness that.

"Camille, this wasn't only sex and you know it. And I know about you because I've been watching you for months now. Hell, maybe even years. You don't leave the hospital with anyone, ever. You're on call more than any surgeon I've ever known. Your life is cutting people open and you do it better than anyone, but you can have more."

"I don't need more."

"Do you want more? Because it sure as hell felt like you did for the past three hours."

Was that how long it had been? Three hours. In some ways it had felt like a lifetime. She strove for a casualness she didn't feel. "I don't want a relationship if that's what you mean. This was fun. But this was it."

"You are such a liar." He was angry. She could see it in his eyes and hard jaw.

"You can't understand that a woman might not want to be in a relationship with the great and almighty Dr. Wyatt Holladay, is that it?"

"No," he snarled, moving into her space. "I can't understand why after three hours of the best sex you have ever had—and don't even try to deny that—you're pulling this act. We have a chance here, Camille. We can be happy. Don't let your hang-ups get in the way of that."

Hang-ups. He had no idea.

"Are you still going to look at those cases I gave you?"

He turned away from her then and she could see that he was biting his tongue to stop himself from saying what he wanted to. "Yes, I'm going to look at the cases."

"Thank you."

"No," he said as he gathered his shirt and shoes. "Thank you. You're one heck of a good lay."

It was supposed to hurt and it did. She wrapped her arms around her body and held tight in case there was more.

He was at her bedroom door when he stopped. "I'm sorry. I didn't mean that. I'm pissed at you, Camille. Royally pissed. And this, whatever the hell it is, is not over."

She didn't move as she heard him pound his way down the hallway. She didn't react when she heard him slam the front door. It wasn't until Aphrodite found her and started curling around her ankles that she began to shake.

She shook for minutes until the numbness settled in.

Chapter 5

Camille left the hospital the next day with an immense sense of relief. Success. She had avoided Wyatt Holladay for ten hours. It had not been done without a degree of difficulty. As immature as it had been to want to evade the man she'd slept with last night—although she was sure women did it every year after office holiday parties—she told herself it was a necessity.

Maybe tomorrow she could face him. Maybe tomorrow if he cornered her and asked her why she threw him out of her home after some of the most intense sex she'd ever known, she could explain it. Maybe.

But not today.

Instead, today she'd broken several self-imposed rules. Rather than being at the hospital an hour before surgery to avoid any chance of a delay in her schedule, she'd waited until the last minute to show up in the O.R.

Plus she'd arrived already dressed in a pair of scrubs

rather than her typical business attire. The locker room where she changed each day was too close to the clinic where Wyatt worked.

Camille could almost hear her grandfather's severe voice in her head.

Dressing appropriately for work is a sign of respect for your employer, your patients and yourself.

It was his rule number fifty-six. Despite him being gone now for three years, she had never broken it. She had never broken any of them until today.

Camille strongly suspected that was part of her problem.

Her surgical schedule for the day had helped her avoidance efforts. Back-to-back surgeries hadn't allowed for much of a break in between. She'd barely had enough time to change, scrub in again and return to the OR. A place where she knew he wouldn't confront her. He would appreciate the concentration required to operate and would do nothing to distract her in that room.

Now she was out of the hospital, leaving through the physicians' entrance to where her car was parked, seconds from a true escape. In addition to the relief of having avoided a confrontation, she couldn't help feeling a sense of disappointment.

He hadn't come looking for her. He hadn't sought her out.

She was grateful for that and she was also bereft. Which made her contrary and quite possibly insane and in no way capable of having and sustaining a workable romantic relationship.

Annoyed with herself, she started to let the door behind her swing closed.

"Hey, Dr. Larson."

Turning at the sound of the voice, Camille was relieved

when she spotted Ruby running behind her. She wasn't necessarily up for another round with her boss, either. The conversation she'd had yesterday with Delia regarding her role in Logan's departure hadn't sat well with Camille. That she'd earned her employer's disapproval was clear. Whether it was justified or not. The only other person she could remember disappointing before was her grandfather.

He was a man who set the bar very high.

She held the door for Delia's assistant and waited for the girl with the too vibrant tan to catch up.

A sudden thought occurred to Camille. "Ruby, tell me truthfully, how is Delia holding up under all the pressure?"

"You've seen her," Ruby replied, hitching her purse over her shoulder as they both made their way down the cement stairs toward the paved lot. "She's crazy. Everything she wants, it's ASAP. She's shouting more than ever, demanding more than ever. I used to think I liked my job. Of course, you giving Dr. Dade the heave-ho did not help."

Camille stopped. "I didn't fire the man. He chose to leave. That is not my responsibility."

"That's not the way most people see it. And when he and Delia were hooking up… Well, let's say she was a lot mellower and easier to deal with."

It took a second for Camille to process what the assistant had said. "Wait a minute. You mean Dr. Dade, Dr. Logan Dade was…was…"

"Shagging the boss?" Ruby supplied. "Uh, yeah. Every-body knew it."

"No wonder she's been so annoyed with me."

At first, Camille had taken Delia's sudden coolness as a joke. Like she was only pretending to be mad that Dade had left. But yesterday, it became too real. Surely a reasonable, intelligent woman wouldn't hold Camille at fault for Dade's ego. But if she'd been sleeping with him, that changed everything. Reasonable, intelligent women could become irrational and mindless when their hearts were on the line. Camille knew that for a fact.

"She never said anything to me," Camille muttered.

It wasn't as though she could call Delia a friend. Camille really couldn't call anyone a friend. She chose to isolate herself and it worked. Still, sometimes she sat at the same table with Delia in the hospital cafeteria. Other times they talked about shoes. That was sort of like a friendship. At least a fond acquaintance. But Delia never told her that she was sleeping with Logan. Camille was certain that was something two female friends should have discussed.

Unless Delia thought Camille was sleeping with him, too, and she didn't want to know.

"It's not like it was a big deal. Dr. Dade was pretty much banging everyone in this hospital. The man was a legend. And apparently into some pretty kinky stuff. I'm sorry I never had my chance at him, but I couldn't very well take my shot while he was also banging the boss. That's a little too…close for comfort, if you get my drift."

For Camille the idea of sleeping with Dade was nauseating. That was the only drift she needed to catch.

Ruby looked at her with an admonishing expression. "You are to blame for a lot of broken hearts around here. I mean, people were really mad at you. I hate to tell you this, Doc, but some people still— Oh, wow. That is messed up."

They had reached the first row of parking spots. Camille already had her automatic starter in her hand. As she approached the engine roared to life but then she saw exactly what Ruby had so accurately described.

It was, in fact, messed up.

A brutal, ugly, gash ran along the side of her silver

BMW. Her windshield sported a crack that hadn't been there when she parked it that morning. Moving around the vehicle, trying to absorb the impact of what was done, she saw a sister streak on the other side dug into the paint.

"You got keyed. That isn't right. I don't care how pissed off people are at you, taking it out on a Beemer is flat out insane."

It took a second for Camille to clear her thoughts and process what the girl was saying.

"Ruby, no one did this to me. It was a kid. Some vandal." Camille studied the damage. She didn't want to believe that anyone could harbor this much anger toward her. To be the target of so much rage, it wasn't right. She had done nothing to warrant it.

"If you say so. But how come none of the other cars are trashed? Sorry, Doc, this looks like someone is still not over Dr. Dade in a serious way."

"But he left a month ago," she said, more to herself. "If anyone was that in love with him, why didn't they continue to see him? City General isn't even a half hour away from here."

Ruby moved close and ran her finger along one of the key scrapes. "You know how it is, Dr. Larson. You start somewhere new you want a clean break. Dr. Dade has moved on and someone has decided to take it out on you."

"Who?" Odd, Camille thought. For a second Wyatt's name floated through her head. He seemed this angry last night. This hurtful. But as soon as she thought of him, his name disappeared. Confronting her face-to-face was more his style.

This sneak attack wasn't him at all.

"Don't know. Like I said, there are plenty of candidates. See you, Doc. Good luck with the car."

With that the girl practically skipped away. Thank goodness she was leaving for the day. The news of Camille's car vandalism wouldn't spread like wildfire until first thing the next morning.

As she made her way home, Camille had to tilt her head to avoid the crack that ran through the windshield. She'd call the insurance company when she got home, but she wasn't going to the police. To call them would make it seem too real. As if Ruby had been right about someone doing this to her maliciously. Camille thought about Delia and Logan and wondered how much the hospital CEO had been impacted by the end of their relationship.

Had Delia had wanted to pursue the relationship outside of work? It wouldn't have been easy for her. The woman hadn't left the hospital before 10:00 p.m. for the past month and she was there most weekends. Much like Camille. If she was seeing someone, they weren't spending a great deal of time together. And it wasn't like Logan to change his schedule to accommodate someone else.

Then again, quickies, by their very definition, didn't take a lot of time.

Camille shuddered with the memory of what one of those looked like.

She'd caught Dade once in the on-call lounge. A quiet spot with two beds where a doctor could catch some sleep. He'd had Marie, a surgical nurse, cornered up against the wall. Her back to him. It had been rough and quick with a great deal of grunting. Mid grunt Dade had turned his head, aware that someone had entered the room. He'd smiled at Camille. It had been smug and twisted and it sent her flying out of there faster than if the floor had been covered with spiders.

The thought of Delia being a partner in that made her sad. Realistically, Dade had probably ended their affair as soon as she was no longer useful to him. Camille had no problem imagining Logan using Delia for what he could get out of her. She only hoped that Delia hadn't realized his true purpose.

And she hoped she hadn't been one of those women in the on-call lounge. An intelligent, driven woman who ran a hospital shouldn't be used that way. As nothing more than a body with her face pressed into the wall.

The next day Camille entered the hospital determined to put the vandalism out of her mind. She would let someone in administration know what happened, of course. They might want to post a warning on the message board in the staff lounge regarding being on the lookout for a vandal in the area.

That was only courteous. It also made it less about her in particular.

She'd made the appointment with her dealer to get the car fixed and was now driving a loaner. She hated the idea of knowing that if someone had done this to her on purpose they would see how she'd been inconvenienced. She hated knowing that this might have been done to her at all.

First, Delia's disapproval. Now, someone's irrational anger aimed at her. These weren't things Camille was used to dealing with. She had no skill set to combat it.

With her grandfather it had been easy. She needed to live up to his expectations. A difficult but clearly defined goal. How did someone fight an enemy she couldn't identify? Or deal with anger that was unjustified?

It was vexing but ironically it wasn't the car that bothered her most last night as she lay in her bed not sleeping. Thoughts of Wyatt filled her head and she'd been unable to eject them.

He hadn't tried to contact her yesterday.

When she'd gotten home and had time to think about it, she thought it was strange he hadn't sought her out at least once. Despite her tactics, he could have found her if he really wanted to.

He could have called her.

Someone had vandalized her car, and even though there was no possible way he could have known that, she thought how soothing it would have been if he'd called to see if she was all right.

Of course he was angry with her and that's probably why he left her alone. But she had been planning for the confrontation. Expected it. Had worked hard to avoid him.

Unless, he didn't care anymore.

Camille pushed open the door to the hospital locker room. It was a co-ed facility, but most took it for granted that the women stayed toward the right and the men the left. Not that most doctors cared if they got caught in their underwear. Bodies were just that to doctors. Big, small, skinny, fat. Once you've seen one naked on an operating table with a chest split open, it took most of the mystery out of them.

Still, Camille preferred her privacy. Her locker was tucked in a corner where she was hidden from view. She shrugged out of her suit jacket and slid the zipper of her matching skirt down. Standing in the practical, beige bra and panty set she'd put on that morning—a set that basically matched every other one she had—she carefully placed her clothes on the hanger inside the locker that bore her name.

The other night she hadn't thought about putting on something sexier under her cocktail dress. There was no thought in her head that dinner might lead to sex. A normal woman would have, she knew. A normal woman would have realized the chemistry that existed between her and Wyatt even if their opinions on everything else differed. A normal woman would have been prepared with black lace. Just in case.

Camille was not normal.

She sank onto the bench, her scrubs in her hands, and waited for the wave of anger and hurt to overtake her. She was so damned afraid all the time.

Dr. Rosen had said it was her mother's fault for abandoning her. Or her father's fault for not being able to handle the responsibility of a baby being left with him. Mostly it was her grandfather's fault for regimenting her life too much. Her grandfather who raised her to be everything that she was.

The most gifted thoracic surgeon on the East Coast.

And the most socially inept woman any man had ever known.

Camille took a deep breath and tried to push it out of her mind. It was in these moments of blame that she became angrier with herself more so than her parents or grandfather. They had had an impact on her life. There was no debating it. But it was within herself to change if she wanted to.

She could have walked to her bedroom where Wyatt was getting dressed. She could have said that she loved pizza with meat on it. They could have drunk some wine and soda water, eaten greasy food, laughed about the disaster of their first date and made love again.

She could have done that if she wanted. But she didn't.

Why?

Camille thought of the rules it broke. *Don't get involved with a coworker. Don't let personal relationships distract you from the work at hand.* In the end, it hadn't been her grandfather's rules that had her freezing up. It had been fear. She only wished she knew where the fear came from. She despised not knowing the answer to any question.

With all the pent-up anger inside her she slammed the locker door shut and watched as it rattled in its frame.

Wyatt leaned against a row of lockers, watching Camille, unsure of how to approach her. He'd spotted her immediately. As soon as she'd walked through the hospital's main entrance doors. For very good reason. He'd been waiting for her. But she appeared distracted and unaware of anything or anyone around her. There had been a look about her, a vulnerability that had made him deviate from his plan.

Yesterday he avoided her.

After being evicted from her bed and her home, he'd spent the rest of the night thinking about how he'd threatened her that what they had wasn't over. The anger about what she'd done, what she'd so casually thrown away.

What was so great about Camille Larson? Why did he need the hassle? What sane man would put up with a woman with all her quirks when she'd shoved him out of her bed?

So he'd gone to work, done his shift in the clinic and not once had he walked the corridors searching for even a hint of her.

By the time he'd gotten home, he'd been nearly crazed with frustration. He wanted to see her. Talk to her. He wanted to kiss her. Tell her that she was driving him nuts.

He wanted to hold her. And he damn sure knew that he wanted her in his life. Hassle or no.

Today was supposed to start out with dragging her

kicking and screaming into the nearest treatment room
and shouting at her until she began to see reason. He had
all these angry things he wanted to say. That she was a
child and it was time for her to grow up. That she couldn't
hide herself within the confines of the hospital for the rest
of her life. That they had a shot at a good thing and she
was blowing it. She would regret it.

But when he saw her looking the way she did, as if
she was lost in the middle of the place she knew best,
he stopped himself. Instead he followed her. Now, as he
leaned against the metal walls, watching her sitting there
in her underwear, he thought about how much of what had
happened had been his fault.

He'd been a fool to push her so fast. She wasn't prepared
for what happened between them. That was obvious. He
should have sensed that after the first time they made love
and maybe have even slowed things down then. Let her get
used to him, to the intimacy of it. Instead he'd turned her
over and took her again. And again.

It had to have been an overload of all her circuits, both
sensual and emotional. He was confident of that fact
because it had been that way for him. And he wasn't nearly
the loner she was.

His poor Camille. He'd devastated them both in his rush
to have her and now he was faced with the truth. Yelling at
her and shaking her until she admitted how she felt about
him was not going to help. He needed a new approach.

"So what did the locker door do to piss you off?"

She startled. He wished he hadn't done that. Immediately,
she was on her guard. She stood and blushed as soon as
she saw him. She hadn't put on her scrubs yet, so she tried
to cover herself. It was pointless. She could be layered in
Eskimo furs and for the rest of his life he would see only

the naked Camille who had been stretched out on the bed underneath him.

"I—I didn't…see you."

"You look upset about something."

"I suppose you heard from Ruby?"

"I haven't heard anything from Ruby."

"Oh. Well, it's nothing."

She was a lousy liar and he thought it charming. He was so gone over her. "I want to apologize for the other night."

He read her confusion.

"I wanted to take you to dinner. I wanted to have a chance to get to know you better. I pushed things and I'm sorry."

"I let you," she answered frankly.

"You did. But still, I'm sorry."

"I told you to leave. You were angry. You had every right. I didn't even let you have pizza. Why are you apologizing?"

Because you look like a frightened cat backed into a corner and the only way to approach you is slowly, cautiously and without threat. "Because I am. I should have brought you flowers. We should have gone out. Maybe dancing."

"I don't dance."

Wyatt closed his eyes struggling for patience. "Are you on call tonight?"

"Yes."

"You're on call a lot."

"I prefer to work."

"Why don't I cook you dinner? I've started to review the cases you gave me. We could go over what I've found."

She shook her head. "I already told you I'm on call. I have to be close."

"My place is only a couple miles from the hospital. As close as yours is but in a different direction. What do you say?"

Instead of answering, she bent over and stepped into her pants. She pulled the cotton jersey over her head quickly. He got a flash of belly button which reminded him of when he'd tongued her there and she'd moaned as if he'd been much lower on her body. He closed his eyes and suppressed his own groan.

"You want me to come for dinner?"

"Dinner. Nothing else. We'll review the cases and that's it."

"Why?"

He wasn't sure what she was asking so he went with the more obvious answer. "I promised you I would look over them and I'm keeping my promise."

She looked away and there again was that look. It screamed for him to tread softly and so he would.

"Just dinner."

Victory, he thought. He was so relieved he wanted to shout. But he didn't. "I'll do burgers."

"I prefer fish."

He hated fish. "I'll do fish."

"Okay."

"Okay." He sighed. "I'll write the directions. You can call when you're on your way."

It was hard to do but he turned and walked away. He wanted to show her that he had no plans to crowd her or push her again. Camille Larson was no ordinary woman and he was going to have to respect that and alter his actions accordingly.

Quite frankly, he wasn't sure why it was so necessary for him to involve her in his life. She was prickly, a workaholic, close-minded about things he wasn't and downright difficult.

And she was coming over for dinner tonight and he was so happy he whistled.

Chapter 6

Camille got in the loaner car she was still getting used to and hesitated before starting it. Gingerly she bent her neck and sniffed herself. The scent of the expensive lotion she'd applied before leaving the house taunted her.

She'd told herself this dinner was going to be about the cases. She promised herself that she would let nothing happen other than a professional conversation and a shared meal. She convinced herself that after throwing him out of her house, the last thing Wyatt would want was a repeat performance.

Then she'd gone and changed her underwear and applied the scented lotion. An extra dollop between her breasts.

Shaking her head, angry with herself, she slowly reversed out of her driveway. Wyatt lived in the next town so it wouldn't take her long to get there. Which meant she had to use every minute of driving time to go over in her head what this night would be about.

Business.

Advice.

A meal.

One that he was cooking for her. Fish, he promised, because that's what she liked. Which was really sweet of him now that she thought about it. He was a red meat eater. The last time they had gone out, she tried to explain to him the impact on his heart that too much red meat would cause when he'd ordered a New York Strip steak. He had ignored her facts and devoured the steak.

Sensing a vehicle approaching from behind, Camille checked her rearview mirror, but the car had quickly slid around her and passed her on the left. They weren't on a highway but a two-way stretch of road, which meant the car on her left was actually driving on the wrong side of the street.

Glancing over she saw nothing but black paint and tinted windows before the car was speeding past her then moving to the right to cut her off. She couldn't imagine what kind of hurry the driver was in that warranted such reckless driving. Even had she been called into the hospital for an emergency surgery she wouldn't have driven like this.

Before she could formulate a realistic scenario for what was happening Camille saw red brake lights in front of her.

Instinct had her slamming on her brakes and, true to its advertising, the luxury vehicle stopped on a dime. She heard the squeal of the tires gripping the road and waited for impact. Her body was thrown forward with the abrupt stop, then snapped back with the pressure from the seat belt. At some point she closed her eyes. When no collision occurred, she opened them to see the car speeding far down the road. It made a right at the next light and was out of sight.

Pulling over to the side of the road she put the car in Park. She needed a few minutes to catch her breath and let the adrenaline that was flooding her system recede.

What in the hell had that been about? Perhaps something had passed in front of the driver? A squirrel? Regardless, the person was a menace. If she spotted the car again, she might get a license plate number and report the driver. For now, there was nothing left for her to do but resume her journey.

When Wyatt opened the door to his town house Camille had the strangest inclination to fall into his arms. Ruthlessly she suppressed it. Nothing had happened. There was no reason for her to still feel so jittery. Certainly no cause to wrap her arms around Wyatt's waist and rest her head on his shoulder. No cause at all.

Lifting her chin, she tried for a polite smile. "Hello, Wyatt. I smell fish."

"Exactly what every man wants to hear when a woman enters his home," he said, returning her smile. "Remember, the fish was your idea."

"This isn't half bad," Wyatt said after a bite. Not that he was touting his own cooking skills, but the fish he'd been forced to buy was actually edible.

"Sea bass. It's my favorite."

And expensive as hell, he thought. Why anyone would pay that kind of money for something that wasn't filet mignon he wasn't sure, but she seemed to like it, which was all that mattered.

He'd offered her a glass of wine to go with it. Wyatt believed that because he was an alcoholic didn't mean he couldn't offer a guest a drink. It had been strange for him to be in a liquor store. He realized it was the first time he'd been in one since he'd gotten sober. For a second he wondered if he would be bombarded by temptation, but all he really had been thinking about was how many glasses of wine it might take to get Camille back in bed.

Bad Wyatt.

Then the colors of the liquor bottles around him began to grow a little shiny and pretty. He bought the wine and got the hell out of there. Still, he was glad he'd done it. One less thing to be afraid of. A damn liquor store.

The irony of it was it had been a useless task. She'd refused the wine because she was on call. She could use it though. She was as jumpy as a cat. He assumed it was because she was nervous about being with him again. He couldn't say he blamed her. The last time, he hadn't waited an hour before taking her to bed. Which is why he planned to take this night as slowly as he could. He hadn't kissed her, hadn't put his hand at the small of her back when leading her to the dining area. Hadn't done anything remotely intimate or physical other than pull her chair out for her.

It was driving him crazy. Worse, it wasn't working. Because she was still nervous and fidgeting. So much so that he found himself asking her flat out.

"What's wrong?"

The fork in her hand dropped and clattered on the plate. "What do you mean?"

"I mean that. You're trembling. You have been since you walked through the door. I'm not going to pounce, you know. This is dinner and some work."

"I know," she said, wrapping her arms around her waist. Then she deliberately released herself and set both hands on the table. "I know. It isn't what you think. It's not you."

"It sure as hell is something."

"It's silly. I was almost in a car accident on the way over. I guess I'm still a little shaky from it."

He reached his hand across the table and took hers. "Are you all right?"

In a blink she snatched her hand back. Then seeing what she'd done, she bowed her head. It was as though she was disgusted with herself. "I'm sorry. I don't know why I do that."

"You're a germaphobe who doesn't like to be touched," he offered.

"*Germaphobe* is not a real word. I saw you wash your hands before serving me. That was nice of you."

"I aim to please. Forget why you pulled your hand away. It was instinct."

"Not a good one."

Wyatt stood and walked around the small four-top he called his dining room table. In reality it was the only table in the house. He stood in front of her chair. "Let's get back to my original question. Are you all right?"

"Yes. I'm fine. Some crazy driver. I nearly collided but I didn't."

"Stand up."

She looked at him cautiously. "Why?"

"Stand up." If he told her what he was going to do, she wouldn't agree. Better to simply command it. After a second she stood, the paper napkin she'd properly put on her lap fluttering to the floor.

He eased forward. He slid his arms around her waist and gently brought her into his body. "Sh, you're okay."

He thought he heard her sigh and then he felt triumphant as she wrapped her arms around him and rested her head on his shoulder.

"This is nice," she mumbled into his shoulder.

"You had a scare. Everybody needs a hug after a scare."

"My grandfather used to say scares were silly."

That was interesting. It was the first time she'd ever referred to a family member. Wyatt wanted to press her for more information yet he was leery to ruin the moment. But since this was the first opening she'd ever given him, he took it.

"Grandfather, huh? Did you spend a lot of time with him growing up?"

"He raised me." As she said the words she pulled away from him.

Still, Wyatt thought he had made progress. She had hugged him and let him hold her for nearly two minutes.

"I'm going to get you a glass of wine."

She shook her head. "I told you I can't. I'm on call."

"A half a glass then. It won't intoxicate you and you need something that will settle you. Nobody wants a shaky surgeon operating on them." Wyatt walked to the kitchen and opened the refrigerator where he'd stored the pinot grigio. He uncorked it and splashed two fingers in a wineglass for her. She had followed him into the small kitchen and leaned against the counter. He handed the glass to her and waited until she took a sip.

"What happened to your parents?"

For a second he didn't think she was going to answer. She took another sip of the wine and set it aside.

She didn't look at him when she spoke. "My father got my mother pregnant. They were very young. She didn't want me and gave me over to my father. My father couldn't handle the pressure of a baby so he left. My grandfather raised me. Simple."

Hardly. "I see."

"My grandfather was a surgeon. A brilliant one. He thought his chances of grooming his son to take over his legacy were gone, but then I came along."

"Are you still in touch with your father?"

"Christmas cards. Birthday calls. That sort of thing. He works for a cruise line. Spends his life sailing the world. He's happy."

Pieces. Lots of different pieces to the puzzle that was Camille and finally they were all starting to come together. "You said your grandfather thought scares were silly. What does one do with a little girl who hears things go bump in the night?"

He'd meant it as a casual joke. Little girls were always squealing about something, weren't they? Spiders and bugs. Mice and scary shadows in the dark. But he could see her go to a place in her head that wasn't pleasant.

"He didn't like to be woken in the middle of the night. If I had a bad dream, I had to deal with it. Rule number twenty-two—you have to conquer your fear. If you can't, then you should be ashamed."

It sounded like she was quoting from a medical text. Wyatt knew that's how it must have happened, too. Her grandfather's solution to a bad dream was to tell her to conquer the fear and, if she didn't, she should feel shame. Fear and shame mingling together in a little girl's mind while she sat in the dark. Alone. Afraid.

"Where is your grandfather?" Because when Wyatt met him he was going to kick his ass even if he had to pull him out of a wheelchair to do it.

"He died three years ago. Congestive heart failure."

"I'm sorry."

She shook it off. "I don't really like to talk about him. Wait, that sounds awful. I loved him, of course. And he was an exceptional mentor. I wouldn't be the surgeon I am today without him."

A *mentor?* Had he raised her or groomed her?

"You were with him from the time you were a baby. How does one mentor a baby?"

"I really don't want to talk about it. Please. I'm fine. I feel much more settled now. Thank you for the wine. You were right, it helped."

The wine, not the hug. Wyatt wanted to call her on it, but he could see she was already in defensive mode level two. If she got to level three, she would split.

"Okay. We should talk about why you came over then."

"The cases." Her eyes lit up and he could see that she was relieved to have a subject she could embrace.

"I've studied them backward and forward."

"Did you have to speak to the families?"

"I did. I wouldn't have considered it a thorough job if I hadn't. I made it seem like the hospital was doing a routine follow-up. And I spoke to Chuck."

"Dr. Montgomery. The medical examiner."

Wyatt nodded. "He said the autopsy revealed nothing conclusive. There was no leakage…"

"Of course there wasn't. I told you the surgeries were perfect."

"You also asked me to check every angle."

"Every other angle besides a surgical mistake. Because I didn't make one."

Wyatt nodded indulgently. "And I spoke to Jeff and Marie."

Jeff had been the surgical nurse for Mr. Morose. Marie for Mr. Moss. It made sense that he would speak with them, but she couldn't imagine how they might comment on the surgery. "You think they could tell you something about those operations that I couldn't?"

"Frankly, yes. A surgical nurse's job is to stand by your side. Jeff and Marie would have the best view if you had messed up."

Camille slapped her hand on the counter. "I can't believe this. You're questioning me? My talent?"

She wouldn't have been this angry if he were questioning her womanhood, her ability in bed…hell, her entire personality. But call out her talent and his frightened little cat became a fierce tigress. It was sexy as hell, but that was a distraction right now.

"You told me to look at everything," he reminded her. "Everything."

"I thought you believed me," she said tightly. "I wouldn't have lied if I had made a mistake. I would never lie about that."

"Honey, I know you didn't make a mistake. Jeff and Marie both said nothing unusual happened in either surgery." Then again, neither of them could say without a doubt that the deaths hadn't been caused by some mistake. Only it wasn't a mistake either one of them made. So they claimed. Between the two of them, they were more worried about covering up their asses than they were about assuring him that Camille had done nothing wrong.

"What is it?"

"Nothing."

"You made a face when you mentioned Jeff and Marie," Camille accused.

"I got the impression…"

"Marie is probably upset with me."

"Why do you say that?" That was the impression he got. From both of them really. It had been as though they were secretly pleased that he was even questioning the surgery. Jeff and Marie were not fans of Dr. Larson. Marie especially acted as if she had a grudge against Camille.

"Because she was sleeping with Logan. I caught them in the on-call room once. Marie is a highly skilled surgical nurse. She has a great future. I don't know why she would let herself be used like that."

Wyatt didn't figure now was a good time to remind her how good sex felt. It would only put her on edge and that was the last thing he wanted. Not when he'd gotten her to come here. Not when he'd been able to smell the scented lotion on her when he'd held her in his arms. He also didn't want to make any comparisons between what Logan did with his women and what they had done together.

"Did you know Delia was sleeping with him?"

Wyatt shrugged. "The whole hospital knew. It wasn't like Logan to hide his conquests."

"I didn't. I thought Delia and I were friends. I thought… It doesn't matter. But according to Ruby, Delia and the rest of the hospital all blame me for Logan leaving. So it's no surprise that people aren't going to go out of their way to back me up."

"Hey," he said, lifting her chin with his knuckle and looking into her eyes. "I'm backing you up."

"You are. But you said yourself there is nothing there. No obvious reason why those two men died."

Wyatt had to agree. He couldn't find anything in their histories. He couldn't find any type of infection or medication issue. He didn't see anything on the medical examiner's report and he trusted Camille completely when she said there had been no complications during surgery.

"Do you trust me?"

Camille blinked a few times, which wasn't the best answer. "Medically speaking…yes."

Also a sucky answer. "I have one last suggestion."

"Go for it. Anything that might help explain what happened."

"I want to dig them up."

Chapter 7

"You want to dig up bodies?"

Sheriff Mooney, the head of the police department in Westend, the town where the hospital resided, leaned back in his chair with his fingers steepled. He looked like a man whose day was about to get more interesting. In a small suburban hamlet, the township cops' energies were mostly spent on teen vandalism, underage drinking—which caused teen vandalism—breaking up parties where teens could be found drinking underage and speeding tickets.

Digging up dead bodies was not the norm.

"I believe the appropriate term is exhumation," Camille interjected.

Wyatt put a hand on her forearm reminding them of their deal. This time he would do the talking. Camille had a tendency to use words people didn't know, especially when she got nervous or was trying to make a case. For some it was off-putting. To him it was another piece of her puzzle.

"I know what the proper term is, thank you. Do you have any idea what's involved in exhumation?"

Wyatt looked at Camille. "Uh...not really."

"Not really? Exactly," the sheriff drawled. "There are these things called laws that we have that dictate this kind of stuff. But we'll get into that. First, tell me why you want to do it."

Wyatt took a deep breath and prepared to deliver the speech again. They had already struck out with both families, although he pretty much blamed that on Camille. She spoke in a language they didn't understand and, at the end of the day, satisfying her medical curiosity wasn't enough for them.

Appealing to the sheriff to allow the exhumations was a last-ditch effort.

"Look, two men died in our hospital of causes unknown."

"You said they had heart surgeries."

"Specifically multiple bypass surgery," Camille interjected again.

"Right. Did you cut open their chest and reroute some blood?"

"I did."

"And they died," the sheriff concluded.

"Yes, but not because she opened their chests and rerouted blood. That's what we're trying to discover. Those men should have recovered and we would like to know why they didn't."

"And you told me at the start that you had already talked with both families."

"Yes, they were very resistant to this idea." Camille

crossed her arms over her chest as if annoyed. "Irrationally so. They demanded we leave their homes immediately."

"Go figure."

Wyatt wanted to remind her why sometimes grieving widows didn't like to discuss the topic of unburying their husbands, but he didn't want to start an argument in front of the sheriff. They needed to appear united if they had a chance of succeeding.

"Sheriff, I know this seems crazy but all we're really after is some answers. What we have are two men with heart conditions that were successfully treated. There is no substantial reason for their deaths post-op. We want to take another look."

"These men weren't autopsied?"

"The autopsy was inconclusive," Camille stated.

"Inconclusive. That's a fancy word for nothing obvious," the sheriff said. "So you would have known if there was some drug foul-up or hospital staff infection or something like that?"

Wyatt could see the writing on the wall but he couldn't lie about it. The facts were too easy to check. One call to the medical examiner and he would know everything. "Yes. Any type of mis-dosing should have shown up in the blood work. Certainly an infection would have been detected. There was nothing."

"Oh, there was something," the sheriff announced. "It's called the Hand of God. And He decided those two were ready to go."

"That's preposterous," Camille muttered. "Even if there is a God it is highly unlikely He has hands."

"Look, Ms.—"

"Doctor," Camille corrected.

"Doctor and Doctor, you both know what my answer is. First off, an exhumation can't even be contemplated without the permission of the families. Then you would need a court order by a State Supreme Court judge, which I can tell you isn't going to happen with the proof you've laid out. You have two men who died, who were autopsied, and nothing out of the ordinary was found. End of story. Go back to the hospital and concentrate on saving the lives you can."

Defeated, Wyatt stood and shook the man's hand. "We're not ghouls. We wanted answers and felt we had to follow every possibility."

The sheriff glanced at Camille as if he wasn't too sure about her ghoul status, but then turned back to Wyatt. "I understand. I live around enough of you doctors to know that sometimes you think you can control everything. This one was out of your hands."

Camille's face tightened with that comment, but she said nothing.

Together they left the station that was centered in the middle of the town's main street and headed for Wyatt's Jeep parked on the other side of the road.

"Well that was a big waste of time," Wyatt said as he climbed into the driver's seat.

Once again, Camille was struggling to find a spot on the roll bar she deemed clean enough to put her hand on to lift herself into the seat. Eventually she gave in and used a wipe from her purse.

"It's not that dirty," Wyatt grumbled. "I was off-roading in the Pine Barrens last weekend. It's a little dusty."

"It is not a *little dusty*. It's filthy," she clarified as she settled into the seat. "Do you know how many germs are in dirt? It's filled with bug and animal feces…"

He noticed she even cleaned off the seat belt clips before buckling herself in. He shook his head in exasperation. "Okay, enough with animal feces."

"Sorry, but it's true."

There was a pause between them and he could practically feel the gears spiraling in her head.

"So what happens now?"

Wyatt winced. He was hoping she had already come to the only possible conclusion. "Nothing."

"You mean we're giving up?"

He glanced at her. "Camille, there is nothing else we can do. I can't look at the bodies. I've been over every piece of documentation, all the lab results. I can speculate on a few possibilities, but the point is, without evidence to back them up, they're theories."

She sank into the seat. He knew she was disappointed, but there wasn't any avenue left for them to take. All roads had dead-ended. No pun intended. What concerned him now was the more personal aspect of this mini-investigation.

With her reason for initially seeking him out over, what was going to happen to them?

He'd been careful with her last night. So much so that he thought he'd made some progress. He'd been able to hug her without hauling her over his shoulder and taking her to bed. Which showed he had restraint.

He'd cooked for her, which showed he cared.

And he'd kissed her cheek and let her leave after the evening was over, which showed…he was an absolute idiot. He should have done more to cement their relationship. Hell, he wondered if she even knew they were in a relationship.

Weren't they?

He noticed she wasn't moving, merely staring straight ahead.

"What are you thinking about?"

She shook her head. "I don't know. I guess I'm sorry

those two men lost their lives and I'm never going to know why."

Okay. Still on the patients. That wasn't horrible. It meant she hadn't moved on from him yet.

"I was thinking," he said casually as he thrust the key into the ignition. "Maybe we could go out to eat. There is this new BYOB restaurant in Old Town I wanted to try."

He felt it then. The slow turn of her head toward him as her incredibly intense focus shifted to him.

"What are you suggesting?"

Careful, he thought. Like the surgeon he used to be, he needed to do this very precisely. No jarring moves. "Dinner. Out this time. Because my place still reeks of fish. That's all."

"That's all."

"Why?" He flashed her a rakish smile. "You thinking of something else? Like maybe dessert?"

There was no corresponding smile. No twitch of the lips. Not even a smirk at the immature nature of his innuendo.

"I don't think dinner would be a good idea."

The Jeep was beeping now because he'd put the key in the ignition but hadn't started the engine. Violently, Wyatt pulled it out. He couldn't drive and rage at her at the same time. It wasn't safe. Because as externally calm as he was now, and as patient as he knew he had to be, he could feel where this conversation was going to end up.

Her stubbornness would drive him quickly to anger.

He wasn't pleased with the foreknowledge. In fact, it made him as sad as it made him angry.

"Why not? We had dinner last night."

"We were reviewing patient histories. It was work."

"We were also talking about hospital affairs, my knack

for seasoning, the fact that eating fish isn't the end of the world and your grandfather."

As soon as he mentioned her grandfather he regretted it. She stiffened, folding her hands carefully in her lap.

"Can we get back to the hospital? I have a valve replacement surgery this afternoon and I want to review my notes before I start. Also, I want to visit with Janet directly. She's frightened of the surgery and I want to reassure her."

"You've got time before you have to be there. Tell me why you won't have dinner with me. Tell me. Is it my breath?"

"Don't be ridiculous."

"My aftershave?"

"See, you're being ridiculous. Maybe I don't want to have dinner with you because of that."

"I'm only trying to find out what it is about me that put you off. I know it wasn't my lovemaking."

He could see the pink rise along her neck and cheeks.

Lowering his voice he raised his hand and softly brushed that pink cheek. "It wasn't that, was it? You wanted me as much as I wanted you. Please admit that. I want to hear you say it."

"I...wanted you."

"Want me. Present tense."

"I—I can't." She closed her eyes as though she were bracing herself for impact. When she opened them, she pushed away the hand that he was caressing her neck with. "You don't want dinner. You want dinner and sex."

"Not simultaneously."

"Stop being cute," she scolded. Which, naturally, only turned him on more. "You want these things and I can't give them to you."

"Why not?"

"Because it's not who I am. I don't date. I don't have affairs or relationships. I cut people open. I save lives. That's my work, that's my life."

There it was, he thought. The anger that he had been trying to keep control of. "That's being stubborn. And close-minded. You say you *can't* do all that, but that's not true. You're afraid to have those things in your life and that's an entirely different matter."

"So what? What does it matter if I'm stubborn or afraid or truly incapable of forming a relationship with a man? Either way it would never work between us. I don't have any experience. I wouldn't know how to behave. I wouldn't know what I was supposed to do. At dinner, in bed, at a cocktail party. I wouldn't know to say things girlfriends are supposed to say when you got sick, or know how to be supportive when you had a bad day. I would be useless. So why even attempt it?"

Wyatt tried to hold on to the threads of her tantrum. "What are you saying? Because you've never done something before you can't learn how to do it? You're a surgeon who prides herself on being up-to-date on the latest technologies and practices. I've seen you practice for hours on cadavers."

"Exactly! *Practice.* You can't know how to do something without it and I've never had it. Not when it comes to this. Without practice there is failure, and in this area, with you, I'm not willing to risk it."

"Fine," he shouted. "You don't want to risk it? Then go find someone to practice on and give me a call when that's done."

That made her blink. "You want me to see other people?"

"Sure," he said, lying through his teeth. "See someone else. See ten other people. Practice until your heart's content. But if I find out if you've slept with any of them, there is going to be hell to pay."

She sighed and shook her head. "You're being ridiculous again."

"You're a mature single woman who is into me," he said between gritted teeth as he started the Jeep. "I'm a mostly mature single man who is into you. Way into you. We like each other despite ourselves and are electric between the sheets. But you don't want to pursue this because you think you haven't had enough practice with men and you're afraid you won't know how to say things like 'I'm sorry you had a bad day, dear.' And I'm the one being ridiculous?"

She didn't respond and for that he was grateful. He pulled into traffic and concentrated on the cars in front of him instead of her.

He hoped she was thinking about what she was willing to let go and what was worth trying for.

She needed to get this right. For his sanity, for his freaking heart. She needed to.

Chapter 8

Camille scrubbed her hands harder than was necessary with the bar soap. There was something soothing in the ritual that made it calming even while she rubbed her skin raw. Germs were to be avoided at all cost. Cleanliness wasn't merely a rule before surgery, it was a surgeon's obligation. A pact between the patient whose chest lay exposed and the person who would be putting her hands inside it.

There were many other rules her grandfather had drummed into her head, but this one was the first.

Rule one: cleanliness.

She wasn't to eat without washing, dress without washing. She wasn't to close a book without then washing. Elementary school was forbidden. Nothing more than a cesspool of germs, her grandfather felt that not only could he do a superior job in her education, but he could shield her from the typical contaminants found in a classroom.

The most predominant of these being other children.

No, it had never been hard to isolate the root of her current hypochondriac tendencies. As a child if she sneezed, it was an issue for concern. She was diagnosed and treated as if she had developed a new strain of tuberculosis. Quarantined at times even from the man who should have been nursing her back to health.

Illness was not to be tolerated. Although he'd since stopped operating on patients as his hands had grown too unpredictable, her grandfather often worked with other surgeons in the OR directing them as needed.

Her health affected his health and his health could not be compromised given his responsibilities.

So she washed herself and stayed away from germs of any kind and suffered his treatments for the minor ailments she had managed to contract over the course of her lifetime.

And she never made any friends. And she never had a boyfriend.

She recalled the first time she had let someone kiss her. Another student she'd met in med school. The revulsion she felt violating such a fundamental principle of her grandfather's had her promptly pushing away from the boy and finding the nearest bathroom where she'd vomited.

It would be years before she allowed herself to even think about such things again. School made it easy. So did the long hours of her internship. Becoming a doctor, then a surgeon, left little time for a social life. But after he died, she knew it was time to break out of the shell he had created for her and try to find a way to be normal.

So she got a cat and she learned to sit still when Aphrodite licked ice cream from her fingers. And she scooped kitty litter, albeit with a face mask and rubber gloves that were secured on her forearms with thick rubber bands.

She found another boy to kiss, a man this time, and waited for the nausea to pass. Then she'd let him have sex with her, which had caused another fit of vomiting. But she tried again, this time with a fellow resident. She let him kiss her and have sex with her and she hadn't vomited.

She also hadn't really enjoyed the experience either. It all seemed like so much work to maintain control of her reactions.

But she hadn't had to do that with Wyatt. With Wyatt she'd been so overwhelmed by the pleasure she hadn't been able to dwell on all the rest.

Another reason why pursuing a relationship with him was risky. With him she felt different, not herself. She was having a hard time determining if that was a good thing or a bad thing. Because she couldn't decide, the only smart course of action was to avoid him and the feelings he evoked altogether.

Her grandfather always said if she didn't know in which direction to proceed, then the logical move was to remain still. In the area of romance she'd been remaining still for most of her life. Somehow in this instance that very logical option felt wrong.

Of course she could take Wyatt's advice. Maybe find a way to practice with other men, build up her level of confidence in her ability to handle a relationship. It sounded like a lot of work, and part of her wondered how these other men might feel about it.

Hi, would you mind going out with me so I can become more sure of myself as a woman so ultimately I might be able to have a relationship with the man I really want?

No, definitely not a great opening line. But she would consider it because despite what she'd told Wyatt earlier today, she wasn't quite ready to give up on herself yet. And definitely not ready to give up on them.

Replacing the soap, she rinsed her hands under the water, wincing at the heat hitting her sensitive skin. Jeff, one of the surgical nurses she would be working with today, came into the washroom with gloves in hand.

Camille held a hand out to him while he snapped the first glove into place, then the next.

Peeking up at him, as he was much taller than she was, Camille realized for the first time that he was handsome. Before she'd only ever seen him as a tool she needed to do her job. It's how she thought of everyone in the operating room with her. A supporting cast with her as the star.

He had a strong chin, long narrow nose and high cheekbones. Firm but full lips. In her eyes he wasn't nearly as captivating as Wyatt, but he was the type of man a mature single woman might take an interest in. The type of person she might…practice with.

"Are you okay, Doctor?"

Caught staring, Camille avoided his gaze. "Yes. Sorry. Is the patient ready?"

"Ready and waiting."

Camille made her way into the O.R. It was crowded today with the anesthesiologist, a resident assisting her with the heart-lung bypass machine, an intern observing and another surgical nurse besides Jeff. Camille wasn't thrilled to see Marie, knowing the animosity the woman felt toward her, but she would not let it affect her work.

She nodded to the anesthesiologist who delivered the anesthesia through an IV line in the patient's arm. As soon as the patient was completely under, the respirator line was inserted into the windpipe and preparation to hook up the patient to the heart and lung machine began.

Camille went about her business methodically. She

preferred a quiet operating room rather than filling the space with background music or television. She liked to think there was a rhythm to a surgery, a silent beat that let her know how it was proceeding. Background noise drowned that out of her.

The only sound today was her detailing step-by-step for the intern how she was proceeding and directions to Jeff and Marie. She explained to the intern why they were using a biological aortic valve replacement instead of a mechanical one and gave her opinion of the use of robotics during heart surgery.

Camille was not a fan of robotics, believing they didn't act as quickly as her human hands did when there was problem.

After several hours and a seamless operation, the patient's heart function was restored and the bypass and respirators were turned off. Again, Camille could find no fault in her technique, but knew that she would be making several visits to the ICU to monitor this patient's recovery. The patient was wheeled out of the O.R. to the post-op recovery room where she would stay until she recovered from the anesthesia before being transferred to ICU.

In the scrub room Camille pushed open the swinging door to find Jeff and Marie casually talking as they washed the surgery off their hands. Camille disposed of her blood-soaked gloves in the hazardous waste bucket and joined them at the sinks.

She wasn't unaware that as soon as she did join them their conversation ceased. Marie had been asking Jeff about his plans for his day off tomorrow and Camille would have liked to have heard the answer. Tomorrow was the first time in a long time she would not be on call. Not a bad day to practice date.

"Good job, you two. In there." Camille nodded to both

of them. It occurred to her that she didn't do a lot of that. Compliments weren't something she expected so they weren't something she offered. Being excellent was her job, expecting excellence from her staff was the norm. So to comment on it every time it happened seemed pointless.

However, given the hospital staff's current feelings toward her, she thought a little flattery couldn't hurt.

They both nodded with somewhat confused expressions on their faces. Camille didn't think that was a good sign.

"So, Jeff...um..." Camille realized she had no clue how to start this conversation. Again, something she needed to practice. "Are you seeing anyone?"

"No," he stated flatly, looking at her as if she had suddenly grown two heads.

"Oh. So I...um...was wondering. Maybe, sometime, if you would like to go out for drinks or something. Sometime. Maybe."

"Are you serious?"

It wasn't exactly the response she was looking for. And oddly, he seemed angered by her question. She knew that asking someone else out so she could learn how to be with another man wasn't exactly thoughtful of her, but she didn't think he would guess her underlying reasons.

"I suppose?"

He huffed. "You really are oblivious, aren't you? I know you're a doctor and we're supposed to bow to you, but I won't. You're a fool. And for the record, I think Dr. Dade is ten times the physician you are. I'm out, Marie. See you."

Jeff sidestepped her and left the scrub room without a backward glance. Camille turned and saw the door swinging from his exit and wondered if she had ever made someone angry by asking them out. She was pretty sure this was a first. He called her a fool. She'd never had such a slur raised against her. Worse, he thought Dr. Dade was better at the job. That was an outright lie.

"What did I do?"

Marie came up beside her, drying her hands. "You really don't know?"

"Know what?"

"Jeff plays for the other team." Camille must have made her confusion obvious. "You know...the *other team*." When that still didn't register, Marie said it straight. "Jeff is gay."

"Oh. I didn't know that." Camille flushed. Should she have known that? She didn't spend much time focusing on the personal lives of the people she worked with. Except Wyatt.

Jeff seemed like any other man to her. Given her limited exposure to men in general she wasn't shocked to learn she had not properly identified him as homosexual. Maybe he was right and that did make her foolish.

"Right. Which is why he was probably so cheesed with you asking him out. He's militantly gay. You know, completely out and open with everything. The fact that you didn't know, he automatically assumes it means you have something against people like him. Like you want to believe they don't exist."

"That's not true."

"Don't sweat it. He'll recover. He's been an absolute jerk lately. Anger central all the time. I think someone broke his heart, but he's not talking."

"I can't seem to do the right thing by anyone in this place."

Marie tossed the towel in the laundry bin. "You are persona non grata these days. Dr. Dade has been missed."

Camille recalled the image of Marie with Dade in the

break room. "Can I ask you a question? What was it that you saw in him?"

"Dr. Dade? Uh, he's hot. He's rich. He's got that surgeon arrogance thing going full blast, which, in short doses, is a huge turn-on. And in bed, I've never had better. He used to put his hands around my throat and cut off my air while I came. It was fabulous."

"You mean sexual asphyxiation?" Camille was familiar with the clinical definition but could never associate something so morbid with making love. It was dangerous and potentially life-threatening and…

"A total mind blower," Marie said. "You should try it."

"I don't think so. Weren't you worried? If he cut off your air supply for too long, he could have stopped your heart."

"I know. That's half the fun. The risk. Besides he used to say he was a heart surgeon and that if he stopped my heart, who better than him to start it back up again."

Camille couldn't refute the logic, but the idea of putting her life in someone else's hands that way, someone who treated her so casually, was insanity.

"I've shocked you," Marie said, patting her gently. "Sorry. I figured everybody knew about Dr. Dade and all the kinky things he likes to do."

"I'm not shocked." It was a total lie. Camille was extremely shocked. It put into context what she'd witnessed in the lounge that day. Marie hadn't been a victim of Dade's sexual domination. She'd been a willing partner.

"So I guess he kept things pretty vanilla with you."

"With me? Not with me. I was never with Dr. Dade… like that."

"Seriously? Then why did you go all crazy stalker on him?"

Camille shook her head, not understanding the gist of the conversation. "Marie, you've completely lost me. I was never intimately involved with Dr. Dade and I certainly never stalked him."

"But he said—huh."

"He said what?"

The nurse shrugged. "After he gave his two weeks' notice his car had been keyed and the windshield smashed. He claimed it was the work of someone who couldn't handle being dumped. I don't think he ever came out and said it was you. But he sure implied it. And he gave that as one of the reasons he was leaving. He was hoping...out of sight, out of mind. You know? Anyway, it's all past tense these days. I tried a few times to call him, but he's not returning my texts or anything. Said he wanted a clean break when he left. I guess he meant it. See you, Dr. Larson."

Camille watched the younger nurse leave and thought she had a very different opinion of Dade's departure. No doubt Logan was hoping that out of sight of her might actually make him look like a better surgeon. But the fact that someone had keyed his car, too, couldn't be a coincidence. Either it was the same vandal at work, or whoever was angry with Logan was as angry with her.

Later, sitting in the break room with a weak cup of tea, Camille checked her watch. It was nearly eleven. The surgery had gone longer than she planned, but her patient would have been moved to ICU by now and she wanted to check up on her as soon as she was settled in. Critical care nurses weren't huge fans of having doctors look over their shoulders when they weren't needed but Camille wasn't taking any chances this time. Her head was telling her that the surgery went well. Everything had looked good. Not one stitch out of place.

The lack of evidence of any wrongdoing with the other two patients should have eased her mind that their deaths were merely coincidental and a circumstance of fate. There was no reason to think she had any part in their passing. Which meant she had no real reason to be worried about Janet Hamilton currently in ICU.

Only her gut—something she could never recall listening to before as it went against her grain as an intelligent doctor of science—made her feel worried. That is why the gut was stupid.

The entrance to the break room was suddenly shadowed and Camille looked up to find Wyatt standing there with a grim expression on his face. He was like the King of Gut, one more reason that made a future with them together impossible.

He walked to where she was seated and she knew instantly that he must have heard of the debacle with Jeff. He wore a half smirk, half frown and his eyes said the rest.

"What are you still doing here?" she asked.

"Working until midnight. Taking another doctor's shift at the clinic."

Her bad luck. His lips twitched and she knew, knew for certain the rumors had already begun to spread.

"You told me to do it," she said sulkily.

"I told you to harass a gay nurse?"

For a second it occurred to Camille that she had guessed right. No, it wasn't even a guess. She had looked at his face and had known that he was going to comment about the incident with Jeff. She couldn't recall ever being that insightful with another person before. It was a milestone.

"I didn't harass him, I simply asked him out. He got very angry and stormed off. Marie had to tell me he was gay."

"Marie shouldn't have had to tell you. Everyone knows about Jeff. He's very open about his personal life."

"That would have required me caring about his personal life before. I didn't."

"I see," Wyatt said, taking the seat across from her. "So why this sudden interest in his personal life now?"

Camille dipped her tea bag a few times to avoid answering.

"You know," Wyatt said casually, "if you were going to practice with anyone, I would prefer it to be with someone like Jeff. Then I wouldn't have to worry about the hanky-panky stuff afterward."

"You have no call to be *worried*. We're not even seeing each other."

"But we want to be."

"You want to be," she corrected. But she knew she was lying. Sitting this close to him, smelling a hint of the soap he used, made her remember what it felt like to lie next to him. To have him inside her body.

"You want to be, too, but you're afraid. So afraid you thought you might try dating someone else to get the hang of it so you can be easier with me. I don't know whether to kiss you for that or be mad at you."

If she had her choice, she would have preferred the kissing. She liked the kissing. She missed the kissing. But if she told him that, then he would do it. He would kiss her and then he would want more of her and then the panic would come back. The fear that she wasn't capable of being in a relationship.

What if they were together for a time, happy for a while? What if he ended it? Could she see herself as someone who would scratch his car and break his possessions? No, she was far too practical for that. Still, she had a slightly better insight into why someone would go to such extremes.

Losing Wyatt, if she ever had him, would hurt. Would really hurt.

Avoiding any more talk of kissing, Camille changed the subject. "Do you know the latest rumor is that not only am I responsible for getting Dade to leave, people think it was because I was stalking him?"

"Stalking him?"

"Yes. His car was keyed and the windshield was smashed and people think I did it. Which is ridiculous because I never saw him that way, but even more so because I would never risk my hands on something like breaking glass."

"Of course not." Wyatt smiled.

"Now that I think about it, maybe that's why someone did the same to my car. Maybe it wasn't anger directed at me, but somebody thought they were avenging Dr. Dade. It's all so childish."

Wyatt frowned. "What do you mean someone did the same to your car?"

"A couple of days ago. I was leaving the hospital with Ruby and my car was keyed, the windshield broken. I wanted to think it was a vandal, but Ruby made it pretty clear how unpopular I was around here."

Wyatt was about to say something, but Camille could feel someone rushing toward them. Anytime a person ran in a hospital, it wasn't a good thing. She jumped out of her seat ready to act but stopped when she saw Jeff.

His face was concerned. "Dr. Larson, you need to report to ICU. Stat. It's Janet Hamilton."

"Why? What's happened?" Camille was already jogging after him and she could feel Wyatt close behind her. "A bleed?"

"No," Jeff said over his shoulder as they reached the elevators. He hit the up button, his face tight. "It wasn't a bleed."

"Then what happened?" Camille shrieked, her impatience at the very limit.

"It was her heart. It stopped."

Chapter 9

After an hour and forty-two minutes of attempted resuscitation, including paddles and reopening Janet Hamilton's chest to manually stimulate the heart into beating, time of death was called at 1:22 a.m. Camille was the doctor on record.

All she wanted to do was go home and hide under the bedcovers for the next few days but that wasn't going to be an option.

Delia was waiting for her.

With arms crossed over her chest, she tapped her foot on the floor, making a clicking sound that immediately bothered Camille.

"What the hell happened?" Delia asked as soon as Camille was close enough.

"A patient died," Camille answered dully. She looked around for Wyatt, wondering if he'd decided to call it a night and leave. It was well past the time his shift had ended.

Still, she thought he might have been here. Waiting. She might have even thought about letting him give her a hug. She liked being hugged, she realized.

"Damn it, Camille! Give me answers."

"I don't have any," Camille snapped. "I know I didn't cause her death, but I don't know why she died."

"This is like the others? Should I have been listening to you all along? Should I have brought in outside help?"

Camille could hear the despair in the woman's voice, wondering if she'd compromised the lives of patients for the sake of a grant.

"Wyatt didn't find anything. There was nothing to find."

Delia shook her head. "Okay, well, three patients in one month is not an accident or a coincidence. Either you're doing something wrong—"

"I'm not."

Delia shrugged. "It doesn't matter. I can't have the people from the Heart Health Foundation questioning what's going on in my hospital. And I'm not putting our grant at risk for one surgeon's mistakes. I'm going to call the board, let them know what's happening and ask for suggestions. If we're culpable in these deaths, then we're going to have to accept that."

"You mean if I'm culpable, don't you?"

Delia's jaw tightened. "I'll call the board first thing in the morning. You and your surgical team will be ready. We're going to review every cut and every stitch. Understood?"

Camille laughed harshly. "Oh, I see. Now you want to find out what happened. What happened to keeping it quiet? What happened to that ton of bricks?"

"They tumbled down around you, Camille. There is no keeping this quiet. Not anymore. You might want to try and get a few hours of sleep. You're going to need to be sharp."

Camille watched the woman walk off, the click, click of her heels sounding like little daggers. Daggers Delia was no doubt going to plant in her back.

Not having the energy to make her way home, and knowing how long tomorrow would be, Camille found the nearest on-call room and an empty cot.

She was exhausted. She was numb. She didn't sleep for two minutes together.

"Where the hell have you been!"

The next morning Wyatt was pacing outside one of the hospital's main conference rooms. A panel of surgeons was gathering together to debrief Camille regarding last night's fatality. Camille had managed to take a shower and put on a new set of scrubs. She preferred the comfort of them and she was going to need every advantage to face what was to come. What she wasn't prepared to face was a shouting Wyatt.

"Here," she answered.

"I ran into Delia after she saw you last night. She said she sent you home. I went there after being pissed off that you didn't wait for me only to find you *not* there. I came back and searched this whole damn hospital for you last night."

He'd been worried. He'd looked for her. Her fuzzy brain processed those facts. "I took my scolding from Delia like a good little girl and found an empty cot to try and get some sleep." Tried and failed.

"I thought I checked every on-call room." He ran his hands through his hair. "It doesn't matter. Are you all right?"

No, she wasn't.

"I'm fine." His scowl told her she wasn't a very good liar.

"Camille…" He reached for her, but she stepped back.

"No, I can't handle you being nice to me right now. Let's do this and get it over with. We can talk later if you want."

"I will want. But okay. Not now. I can see you're barely keeping it together and you need to."

She was barely keeping it together, but she hated to know she appeared that way. She needed to project an air of calm confidence. She'd been through these types of panels before. She'd sat on the other side of them. Questioning everything from the size of the scalpel to the type of sutures used. Her professional judgment would be scrutinized and tossed around for debate.

Yes, this was going to be the longest day of her life.

The door opened and Delia poked her head out. "Camille, we're ready for you."

Camille nodded and took a step forward, but stopped when Wyatt matched her step for step.

He tilted his head after reading her expression. "You didn't think you were doing this by yourself, did you?"

She had. The way she'd faced most things throughout her life.

Wyatt grabbed her hand and squeezed. "This time we do it together."

It was the most supported she'd ever felt. Since her grandfather had attended her medical school graduation.

Only it didn't last long.

After hours of grilling Camille felt as if she was under attack by some perverse god who believed she used her gift to take lives instead of healing them. Delia and the other surgeons had systematically questioned the anesthesiologist, the intern—who was as white as a sheet and could do nothing but babble incoherently—and the resident who gave a blow-by-blow of the surgery.

Jeff and Marie both said they saw nothing unusual. However, they both prefaced their comments with the point that neither were surgeons and wouldn't know if something minor had gone wrong or not.

A great support team.

Hour after hour each one was excused until it was only Camille. The panel decided to take a break. Her interrogators apparently needed to stretch their legs, use the facilities and get something fresh to drink.

Camille saw no reason to move from her side of the table. She was a surgeon who could go hours without eating, drinking, sitting or urinating.

These other doctors and administration staff could not.

"Dr. Holladay." Delia addressed him from across the length of the conference table as people moved about the room. It was the natural order in these types of debriefings that the panel occupied one side of the table while the accused sat on the other.

Not that this was supposed to be a true accusation.

"Yes, Delia?" Wyatt hadn't gotten up to stretch either. He didn't get a soda or fidget in his chair. He simply continued to sit next to her.

"I really see no reason for you to be here. Surely Dr. Larson can speak on her own behalf."

"I think you know I have a special interest in this matter." He turned and wiggled his eyebrows at Camille. He was trying to ease her mood, but she was too strung out for it to work.

"Plus," he added. "I'm a former surgeon and I have reviewed the first two cases in detail."

"I understand you used to be a fine thoracic surgeon.

However, the board has asked me to call in somebody else a little more qualified to review these surgeries. An independent eye if you will. He's been gracious enough to come in for this part of the debriefing."

Camille's throat tightened. Someone qualified to review *her* surgery. Someone the board recommended and Delia knew. There was only one possibility and the thought made her sick to her stomach.

Even as the name coalesced in her mind, she could hear a tapping on the door behind her. Ruby, her fake tan practically neon orange in the fluorescent light, peeked in and announced their mystery guest.

"Delia, it's Dr. Dade. He's here. Are you ready for him?"

After a tight nod from Delia, Ruby retreated. The door swung open and Dr. Dade entered the conference room like a man on a rescue mission. He wore khakis, a red polo and a conservative sport coat. He could have come from the club or a long day at the hospital.

Or more likely someone's bed.

His hair was brown and mussed in a way that Camille thought too young for him. He was physically fit with biceps so massive he often had to cut the scrubs he wore so he could flex them. A walking sexual animal with no thought to anything other than his own pleasure.

He shook hands with the other doctors, then went to greet Delia. His boyish smile, tilted head and outstretched arms seemed to be asking Delia for forgiveness.

Hey, I know I screwed you and dumped you. Probably tried to choke you at some point, too. Then left without a word. But we're all good now, right?

Camille could almost hear him saying the words in that oh, so casual way he had. Like nothing he said, as long as he said it with a smile, could be bad. Delia offered him her hand and leaned in to kiss him on the cheek.

No hard feelings apparently.

Then Dade whispered something in her ear and Camille could see the woman flush in reaction. Pulling away from him she stumbled slightly as she made her way to her chair.

Glancing over at Wyatt, who was watching the reunion, Camille could see he was as annoyed by Dade's presence as she was.

"Camille, you obviously know Dr. Dade," Delia said as she made her way around the table. The others in the room once again began to take their seats.

Dade took the open seat on Camille's left. She did not think for a moment that this implied he was somehow on her side.

"Of course," she muttered.

Wyatt leaned over Camille with a serious expression as if he needed to communicate vital information to Logan.

"Hey, Dr. Jerkoff, still going commando under your scrubs?" he whispered sarcastically.

"Why, if it isn't Dr. I-used-to-be-a-surgeon. Commando is the only way I fly," Dade replied with a smirk. "Besides, the nurses like it when I get excited when a surgery is going well."

Camille shuddered. She'd been in surgery with Logan when he'd chosen not to wear anything under his scrubs. A heart transplant that had been very successful and evidently exciting for him. The nurses had giggled through the whole incident. She'd had to hold back from gagging.

What was it about her that made her so much different than other women when it came to this man? It was as if he was wearing a disguise that nobody else could see through but her. She wanted to shout to the world that there wasn't anything substantial underneath the costume but it felt like barking at the moon.

"Delia, what do you think this is going to prove?" Camille asked.

"Dr. Dade has been generous enough to offer a full review of each of your last three fatal surgeries," she said tightly. The other doctors around the table stopped mumbling to each other to listen to the exchange. For a moment Camille could feel their pity.

"I've already had Dr. Holladay review the last two surgeries. At my suggestion over your objection."

Glancing briefly to her right and left, Delia shrugged. "I had no reason to believe you had become negligent then."

Camille took the blow in the chest. She sucked in some air. "I see. But you do now."

Delia linked her fingers together and placed them carefully on the table. "I'm not doubting your abilities as a surgeon. I know the work you've done for us in the past has been exemplary. What I'm questioning is what's happening to you now."

"You're suggesting I've lost the ability to operate and that's why those people died?" It was unthinkable. Her gift hadn't changed in the course of four weeks. Hers wasn't the hand that killed those people.

It couldn't have been.

Rather than answer, Delia countered. "Why did you suggest Dr. Holladay review the cases in the first place? What did you think was happening in your O.R., Dr. Larson?"

Camille opened her mouth and shut it. Why had she gone to Wyatt? Not because of a mistake she made. "I was looking for a true cause of death based on some outside circumstances. Those operations were a success."

"Right up until the patients died, you mean," Dade chimed in.

"Exactly," Delia agreed. "Look, Camille, I understand you are a good surgeon...."

That brought Camille to her feet. A rush of pride and fury and fear was swirling inside her. She wasn't sure how to get the words out, but she did. "I am not a *good* surgeon. I am a great one. And you know it. It was on my talent that this hospital was even considered for that grant."

Delia closed her eyes and when she opened them they were hard and cold. "Maybe that was true a month ago but something has obviously happened. Until we find out what, you need to reassign your surgical schedule. Not that I imagine you will have many patients left willing to be operated on by you when they hear the news. You are hereby suspended until Dr. Dade can review your work."

It was hard to hear anything over the ringing in her ears. Camille was fairly certain she heard the word *suspended* and nothing after that. She fell into her chair, her arms hanging between her knees and she wondered if she was going to pass out. She knew the simplest way to prevent that was to lower her head below her heart but she wasn't sure she had much objection to fainting.

Oblivion had to be better than this.

"Delia, I think you're making the right call."

Camille's head snapped in Wyatt's direction. The right call? He was agreeing with Delia. The fuzzy numbness was quickly replaced by sharp, agonizing pain.

"Thank you, Dr. Holladay. I don't need your permission or approval but your consensus might help Camille accept the situation."

No, Camille thought. That wasn't ever going to happen. She wanted to ask him why. But she didn't have the strength for even that much. She'd heard the term *world collapsing* before. She always thought it a silly use of hyperbole. Right now it seemed very literal.

"I think you misunderstand me. I believe keeping Camille out of the O.R. is the best course of action not because I think she somehow contributed to the deaths of those patients. But because I think someone is deliberately targeting her."

Wyatt felt the room's attention shift to him. Delia's mouth was slightly open, Dade was smirking at him and Camille looked shell-shocked. He hadn't intended to pull a Perry Mason moment, but seeing the devastation in Camille's eyes when she thought he was betraying her forced him to speak up and clarify.

"What are you insinuating, Wyatt?" Delia asked, her tone disbelieving.

"A month ago Dr. Dade left this hospital in dramatic fashion. This caused a great deal of anger to be directed, or should I say *mis*directed at Camille. Since then, three of her patients have mysteriously died. I studied the two first cases inside and out. I wasn't given permission to exhume the bodies, but now that we potentially have a criminal case that decision might be reversed. Days ago Camille's car was vandalized. Then she was nearly in a car accident where the other driver left the scene. Are you sensing a pattern?"

"Her car was vandalized and someone didn't stick around after a near-miss. That's your incriminating evidence?" Dade laughed. "Both of those events could be completely unrelated. And could have nothing to do with the surgeries. You're reaching, Wyatt. Like you do when you're trying to find the answer to a patient's symptoms that don't all make sense. Go back to your crystals and needles and whatever voodoo you like to practice in the clinic. Leave surgical review to the real surgeons."

"Ah, real surgeons. Let's look at the mortality rate then, shall we? Dade's and Camille's. Should we even bother pulling the numbers?"

Dade flushed, possibly because he knew the numbers better than anyone. His survival rate was average. Hers was near perfect. "Statistically speaking, for Camille to have three deaths in one month caused by her hand would be the same as those three patients dying by shark attack. Let's be real here. Something else is going on."

"Unless Camille is having some kind of breakdown," Delia suggested. "It's not the first time we've lost a good surgeon that way."

Wyatt took the hit but ignored it. He was too focused on what actually might be happening. "You've seen the tapes of the surgeries, you've heard from the resident in this case. The medical examiner couldn't find a legitimate cause of death with the first two, what I'm now going to call victims."

"Wyatt." Camille finally spoke up. "That's crazy. You're saying—you're saying someone deliberately killed those people."

"I'm saying that someone is targeting you. For some reason. Dade, there was a rumor your car was keyed and windshield cracked before you left. Any ideas on who might have done it?"

The doctor shifted in the chair. He looked at Delia then at Camille. "No clue. I thought it might have been Camille."

"Try again. You know she wouldn't have been within ten feet of shattered glass."

He sighed. "Let's say I had some…admirers who weren't exactly pleased when I told them I was leaving."

"Any one particular admirer?"

He paused, then shook his head. His eyes never left Delia's face. "No. It could have been any one of a small group of people. I have no intention of naming them without proof. That's all it takes in a rumor mill like this for fiction to suddenly become fact and that wouldn't be fair. They couldn't help their feelings for me. That's not a crime."

Wyatt controlled his instinct to roll his eyes.

"Besides, what does trashing my car have to do with Camille? If whoever it was was pissed because I was leaving, what's that got to do with her?"

"Everybody blames me," Camille said softly. She cleared her throat and tried again. "Everybody thinks I forced you to leave."

"Well, that's a damn lie. Nobody, *nobody,* forces me to do anything I don't want to do."

"Geez, Logan," Wyatt groaned. "You sound like a bad imitation of Clint Eastwood. Is it so far-fetched for people to place the blame on Camille when you practically pointed to her on the way out? Anger toward you could have easily transferred to the person responsible for making you leave."

"So angry that person would kill for it?" Delia asked. "That's where this all becomes so much theater, Wyatt. You can't tell me that a person so upset about Logan leaving would go from wrecking a car to murder. They are two pretty big extremes."

"Yes, big extremes," Wyatt agreed. "Like going from believing that Camille Larson's talent can win you a new hospital wing to thinking that she suddenly can't operate anymore."

Delia bristled but Wyatt had made his point. "And let's also not forget that someone nearly ran Camille off the road. What is that if not an attempt on someone's life?"

"But the driver didn't hurt me, Wyatt," Camille admitted. "Just passed me and stopped suddenly. Then sped off. It could have been anyone for any reason. A kid joyriding in a parent's car. I can't believe someone would go so far as to kill innocent people."

"That's fine," Wyatt said. "Maybe I'm wrong. But I say let's have the police figure it out. We've got two vandalized cars, a near-miss accident and three patients dead after perfect surgeries. I think that might be enough to garner the sheriff's attention. Then we let him do the investigating."

Delia shook her head. "Do you have any idea what kind of media attention that might bring with it? Do you understand at all what I'm trying to do for this hospital?"

Wyatt wanted to shake the woman. "Is that all you care about? The damn money."

"Don't make me sound like some greedy shrew," she snapped. She ran her hands through her hair and managed only to make it frizzier. Then, realizing she was still being watched by the other doctors in the room, she took a deep breath. "I'm trying to build us a new wing. A discreet review of Camille's surgeries is one thing. A police investigation is another."

"Well, I'm trying to find out why three people who shouldn't have died, did," Wyatt countered.

"Then let me do what I was asked here to do. Let me look at the tapes," Logan announced.

Everyone in the room turned to him. Including Camille.

"I'll review them objectively. I've got no stake in this anymore. I'm only here as a favor to the board. If I can't find any problems with the surgeries, then you may have to consider that something else happened to those people. But if I do…"

"Yes." Delia nodded, almost eager for the latter to be

true. "If you do, then we'll simply handle this in-house. In the meantime, Camille, you're to stay out of the O.R."

"You're making a mistake." Wyatt knew it in his gut. Nothing had added up about those two deaths. Not their histories, not the surgeries and not the fact that the patients were recovering before they died. When Camille had told him about the car accident he had thought nothing of it. Why would he? Why would she? But putting that together with vandalism and the deaths...

Yes, it seemed far-fetched. He would be the first to admit it. Murder at Physicians' Memorial? It sounded like something out of a bad soap opera.

But he was a doctor who specialized in diagnosis. Look at the whole patient, at all of the symptoms, even though some might not apply. Because the books say a swollen toe doesn't have anything to do with a runny nose, it doesn't mean a person doesn't have lymphoma.

And because vandalism and murder were two opposite extremes on the crime scale didn't mean they weren't dealing with a psychopath.

Chapter 10

Camille stood as soon as everyone stopped talking. It didn't matter what Wyatt or Delia believed. The end result was still the same. Either some deranged person bent on revenge was killing her patients—which she couldn't accept—or she was unknowingly committing an error during surgery that was responsible for their deaths. Another option she couldn't accept.

Either way, they were all dead. Either way, she was no longer a surgeon.

"Can I go home?"

Delia nodded. "Yes. Logan will begin the review as soon as he can. I'll let you both know what he finds."

Camille walked out of the conference room and headed to the elevators. She stopped when it occurred to her she had no idea which button to push. Up or down. The day—the past two days—had been entirely too long.

Wyatt moved around her and pushed the down button. "You're not going home alone."

The elevators opened and Camille stepped inside without answering. He followed her and they rode in silence to the lobby. She thought about what she had to do. Collect her purse, empty her locker, drive home. It all seemed like too much.

When the elevator doors opened she stepped out then stood there with no concept of how to begin such an onerous task list.

"I'll take you home. We'll find a way to get your car tomorrow. Do you need house keys?"

"I keep one under the planter on the porch," she said without thinking.

"Good enough."

She knew she was being led but she didn't care. She couldn't say that she cared about anything anymore. She was suspended. She wasn't a surgeon. She could not operate. She could not be what she was. What happened to a person then?

Once outside she realized it was already dark. Funny, when she was operating, eight, ten, twelve-hour surgeries meant nothing to her. But that same amount of time being questioned felt like a lifetime in hell.

When they reached the Jeep she noted that he'd washed it at some point. The green paint gleamed in the dark. It was thoughtful of him, but she didn't have the energy to thank him. Instead she climbed in and fastened her seat belt.

He drove without speaking. She could see him glancing in her direction a few times probably wondering if she was going to lose it, but other than that his eyes remained on the road.

They reached her house and she thought of the new task list in front of her. Fall on the bed, sleep until this nightmare passed. That, she was capable of. When they reached the porch it didn't occur to her to tell Wyatt that she had it from here. Instead she let him get the key, let him open the door, let him walk inside in front of her…

"What the hell!"

Startled by his shouting, Camille blinked a few times. Then she realized that Wyatt was running through her house. No, not running. Chasing someone through her house!

Someone had broken into her home. It seemed unreal and took her a second to know what to do next.

"Camille, call 911. Now!" Wyatt shouted the directions to her, but then took off before she could stop him.

The sound of footsteps pounded through the ranch, then the backdoor slammed and slammed again.

Who wanted her things? Why? She didn't keep money in the house or jewelry. She never wore it. There was only one thing of any real value to her at all and that was…

Aphrodite!

Camille went in search of her pet's favorite hiding spot in one of the kitchen cabinets that had a space in the bottom of it where she could climb up. Any time someone delivered anything to her house, that is where Aphrodite would hide until the coast was clear.

Camille left the cabinet empty for her and furnished it with some toys to make the small dark space hospitable. After all, every creature needed a getaway. When she opened the cabinet she breathed a sigh of relief seeing Aphrodite tucked into a tiny ball in the far corner of the dark space.

"It's okay. I'm here now. Nobody's going to hurt you."

She hoped. Satisfied her pet was safe she closed the cabinet then reached for the phone in the kitchen. She took the portable with her as she called 911 then made her way outside to find Wyatt.

He shouldn't have gone running after the thief. What if the person was armed? What if he had a gun?

"Oh, God. Please no."

She listened for the sound of a weapon but heard nothing. Cursing herself for taking the time to check on her pet first. Wyatt was out there chasing a criminal. He needed backup. Hand shaking, she held the phone to her ear as she looked out over her backyard. Her property bordered a small patch of woods and on the other side of that was another block of homes. Scanning the dark she heard the rustle of someone moving through the bushes at the perimeter of the yard. For an instant she stepped back uncertain of who approached.

What if Wyatt was hurt? Whoever this person was, whoever had come back for her, she felt like she could kill with her bare hands.

"Who is it?" she asked and wished her voice sounded more threatening and less of a hiss.

The tall lean silhouette of Wyatt was impossible to miss as he moved closer. "Don't shoot, it's me."

Camille glanced down and realized she'd pointed the phone in her hand like a gun. Not a very effective weapon, but she wasn't feeling particularly rational right now. She wanted to run to him and throw her arms around him and make him promise never ever to do anything so stupid again but noise was coming from the speaker.

"What's your emergency?"

"Someone broke into my house," Camille reported. She gave her name and address to the dispatcher and was assured that a police cruiser from the sheriff's office would be by shortly.

Wyatt stopped and picked up something from the grass. He studied it for a second before making his way to her.

She couldn't see his face in the dark, but he was winded and his shoulders were slumped.

"He got away?"

A sharp nod of the head was all he offered.

She slapped his shoulder. "You shouldn't have done that. You could have been hurt, killed."

"Yeah. You're probably right, but whoever it was, was more interested in escape." He took a few more puffs of air. "I couldn't see anything. A shape, that's all. He dropped this before bolting."

Camille took the item from his hand and held it out. It was a length of rope with a loop at the bottom. Not a common tool for a thief...it was a noose, she realized. Only not big enough for a person's head to fit through. Only big enough for a small animal.

Turning to her right, Camille vomited into the grass. She could feel Wyatt move around her, circling her waist to steady her and cupping her forehead in his big strong hand. She still felt sick. But she also felt safe.

"I told you I couldn't make out any distinguishing features."

"But you keep referring to the intruder as he," the officer who sat in the chair across from the couch noted.

"He, she, I don't know. They ran fast. That's all I know." Wyatt leaned forward on the couch and watched the kid— because anyone with that clean-shaven of a face had to be a kid—take notes. The deputy seemed earnest, but he also seemed fairly new at questioning.

Camille was sitting next to Wyatt completely still throughout the process. So far all the questions had been directed at Wyatt and he was fine with that. He could feel her tension and knew she'd been pushed to her last straw. Her patient had died, she'd been suspended from surgery and someone had wanted to hang her cat. Or at least had wanted to leave a threatening message. She wasn't in hysterics, she wasn't shouting and maybe that was a good thing. Or maybe the silence was worse.

"Can you think of any reason someone might want to harm your pet?" This time the deputy did direct his question at Camille. When she blinked, he prompted, "Maybe a neighbor not happy with the cat using his lawn as a litter box? Someone with a bird that the cat went after?"

Wyatt shook his head. "This wasn't some neighbor with a grudge against the cat."

"Wyatt, don't," Camille said putting her hand on his arm. "You don't know if it's related. We don't know anything. Delia didn't want—"

"Delia wanted to protect her own ass," he snapped. "Deputy, we paid a visit to the sheriff yesterday morning. I want you to pass along a message to him from us. There is another dead patient."

The kid's eyes opened wide and his jaw dropped. "A dead person? You're saying someone is dead?"

"I'm saying that three patients have died at Physicians' Memorial Hospital in the past month and I don't think it was due to their health. These were all patients of Dr. Larson. I want someone to look into the possibility that she is being targeted. Her car was vandalized. She recently had a near-miss car accident. And now someone has broken into her home with malicious intent. Combine that with three dead patients and I think we have more than a coincidence."

"Yeah," the kid breathed. "Totally."

Wyatt closed his eyes. The deputy was no hardcore detective. But he didn't need to be. He needed to report back to his commanding officer and let him handle it. If the sheriff needed reinforcements for this kind of detective work, he would get them. He'd struck Wyatt as a shrewd man. Maybe they didn't have enough evidence to warrant exhuming two bodies, but when everything was laid out, Wyatt had a sense that the older man would come around.

"I have your cell-phone number. Keep it with you and I'll be in touch." The deputy left then and Wyatt closed the door behind him.

"You shouldn't have done that. The sheriff will call Delia and—"

"And what? I'm not playing around anymore, Camille. Someone broke into your house with a freakin' noose. This can't be ignored."

Wyatt ran his hands through his hair when he realized he was trembling. With rage, fear, he wasn't sure what. This wasn't a joke. Someone wanted to hurt her. Bad. And he wasn't taking any chances with that.

"You need to pack a bag." Ordering her around was probably not the best course of action. She might realize any second that he had no business doing so. But he was scared. He'd never been so scared.

For a moment Camille stared at him. Debating in her head, no doubt, whether she would listen to him or kick him out.

"Please," he conceded. "You have a travel case for the cat, right? Get that and her litter box. Plus food and whatever else she'll need. Then pack what you need because you're coming with me."

"Wyatt, I'm perfectly capable of..."

"You're not!" he shouted. Instantly he regretted it because she shrank a little on the couch. "I'm sorry. But you're not staying here. Do you understand what is happening? Some sick SOB wants to hurt you. In lots of different ways. You're not staying here waiting for the next attack. You're coming with me until we get this mess sorted out."

She pulled her knees up to her chest and wrapped her arms around them. "I can't leave my house."

Wyatt knelt in front of her and pulled her hands away from her body, holding them even when she tried to tug them back. "We can't stay here. The back door lock was jammed open, it won't lock properly. It was a lousy lock anyway, but that's not for this conversation. I won't feel comfortable letting you sleep alone here. If we go back to my place, you can have the spare room all to yourself."

Space. Instinctively he knew she would require it. The intruder had violated her security. Delia had done a number on her psyche by taking away from her the one thing she knew how to do. If he'd insisted on sleeping with her, even to have her close, she would feel that she had no control over anything in her life. The other option was to take her some place secure.

"Maybe a hotel…" she suggested weakly.

He could see her mind processing what staying in a hotel room would mean for her, a room that thousands of others had slept in previously. If he took her to a hotel, she'd end up standing in the middle of the room all night doing everything she could to not touch anything.

"If we go to my place, I'll let you pick out fresh sheets from my linen closet. Or you can bring your own. Maybe pack your pillow and a blanket, too."

Finally, she nodded. Together they worked to gather what she would need. Clothes, toiletries, her pillow and favorite blanket. The sheets she compromised on after being assured he washed his linens in scalding hot water.

Aphrodite was slightly more difficult to corral, having been through the trauma of the break-in. While Camille insisted she must have sensed the danger she was in, Wyatt was less likely to believe that the cat knew the fate she had escaped. However, he didn't contradict her. She was moving along, agreeing to each of his directions and eventually he had her and her cat packed up and headed back to his place.

It was near two in the morning when they walked through the door of his town house. Aphrodite, happy to be released from her cage, took off exploring while Wyatt guided Camille to the guest room. He stripped the blanket and sheets then pointed her to the linen closet.

After dropping off the excess bedding in his room he went back to check on Camille and smiled as she made perfect hospital corners out of the top bedsheet.

"You going to be okay?"

She turned and shrugged.

Crazy, he thought, but he liked that she had given him an honest answer. She could have told him she was going to be fine. It would have been a lie, but he would have understood it. Instead she'd given him the truth and he hoped this was a sign of how much she trusted him.

"Get some sleep, Camille. We can talk about all of this tomorrow."

She nodded. "You're going to have to go into the clinic tomorrow?"

"Yes. I switch off with some of the other doctors every other Sunday. I'm scheduled for the seven to seven but I'll find someone to cover me for the afternoon. Or if Delia's been contacted by the sheriff by then, I might be escorted from the hospital altogether."

"She can't blame you for what's happening to me."

"Unfortunately, she's the boss. She can do whatever she wants." Wyatt stepped closer and lifted her chin with his finger. "Don't worry about Delia. We're going to let the police find out what's happening and then all of this will go away. You'll be back in surgery in no time."

Tears formed in her eyes and it nearly killed him. "Whoever is doing this," she whispered. "They've taken everything from me."

He leaned down and gently touched his lips to hers. "Not everything. And nothing that you won't get back."

She smiled and sniffed back her tears. "You're being really nice to me."

"Yes, I am. I would like that noted."

"Except for when you shouted at me earlier."

"I felt like I needed to penetrate the fog."

She didn't respond to that, but asked, "Are you going to be able to work tomorrow on so little sleep?"

Wyatt smiled again. He'd kissed her, although a peck, but she hadn't backed off. Instead it seemed as though she was talking so that he wouldn't leave. They stood together in the intimate confines of the room, with the bed a few feet away, and she wanted him not to leave. It wasn't the same as asking him to stay. And despite his arousal he wasn't inclined to push her.

He had her in his home. She was safe and she trusted him. Given Camille's nature, it was a step that was tantamount to landing on the moon as far as Wyatt was concerned.

"I'll be fine. Doctor, remember? We don't do sleep."

Camille stepped back and rubbed her arms. "I hate to be at loose ends. I can't remember the last time I didn't know what I was going to do the next day. And being in a strange house…"

Wyatt considered that. "Wait here."

He left the room and made his way to the utility closet. Picking out a few items, he gathered them in a bucket he kept there. He startled when he felt the cat wind her way through his legs. Bending down he stroked the animal from head to tail. "You make yourself at home here, okay? And I'll help your mom adjust."

Wyatt returned to the guest room. Camille was plumping her pillow and smoothing out the wrinkles of her blanket. He watched as she ran her hand once, twice, three times over the blanket until it was perfectly smooth. She wasn't a woman who was used to wrinkles in her life. She'd done everything she could to avoid them. And now they were everywhere. Provided not only by the person who wanted to hurt her, but him as well.

"Hey, I thought you might like these."

Camille turned and saw the bucket in his arms. She smiled again and he felt like he'd won the lottery. "You want me to clean your house?" she asked as she eyed the gloves, cleansers, brushes and spray bottles he'd stuffed in the bucket.

"That's the beauty of having a germaphobe live with you. Come on." He shook the bucket. "You know you want to."

She took the bucket from his hands. "You're right. I do."

"You can go to town tomorrow. Tonight try to sleep."

Wyatt was about to leave when she reached out and touched him. Another first, he thought.

"You really think someone killed those patients. Intentionally?"

He wouldn't lie. "I do. And what's really awful is that three innocent people died in order to make you pay."

"Pay for what?" she asked, the shock evident in her voice.

"That's what we're going to find out."

Chapter 11

Camille scrubbed the countertop in Wyatt's kitchen as fiercely as she would her hands before going into surgery. Wyatt's idea to give her cleaning supplies to make her feel more comfortable was genius. Not only did it occupy her for hours, it also showed her that he considered what she would need to feel comfortable in his home.

His home.

Camille stopped her scrubbing and took the time to really look at his space. Comfortable furniture. Muted colors. It was homier than she thought it would be. And she wasn't sure why she was surprised. The Wyatt she'd been attracted to from a distance was cool but easygoing. Friendly to most people around him. And his home reflected that. The Wyatt who occupied this space was comfortable and easy with himself.

It was one of the things she envied the most about him. He seemed to go through life as if he owned it. It should have annoyed her. But then he confessed how that attitude had hurt his career. His life. He pretended that she was the one with all the issues, but there had to have been more fallout for him.

He lost the career he thought he would have forever, maybe for the best, but still it had to be hard. He'd lost his wife. It occurred to Camille he hadn't mentioned her much during their acquaintance. Not that there would have been any reason to, but even back in the days when she was learning from him, getting to know him, his wife wasn't a topic between them.

She thought about how she'd left him. It seemed during his darkest hour. He'd resigned his position as a surgeon and the next day had checked into a rehab facility. When he returned, sober, he'd been jobless and spouseless but with a new purpose in his life. The clinic.

At the time it had been nothing more than a small section of the hospital with a few extra beds. In the past few years Wyatt had made it into something bigger than that. Now the clinic was a vital part of not only the hospital, but the surrounding community as well. A place where someone knew they could go for treatment even if they didn't have the advantage of the best health insurance. From runny noses to broken arms, to the diagnosis of more serious conditions, the clinic was part emergency room and part hometown doctor's office.

The woman must have been a fool to have let him go. Or maybe she'd been too self-absorbed to stay with him while he struggled. Or maybe she'd stopped loving him, but Camille couldn't see how that was possible.

All she knew was that if she had been with him then, she would have fought to hold on to him, no matter how awful things had gotten. Because there was something about Wyatt that you knew you could count on. He was a man who was going to come out on top. He screamed that kind of confidence.

If he fell, he would get up. If he became a drunk, eventually he would get sober. If he was behind, he would come back to win.

Maybe his wife hadn't thought he was good for another comeback, but Camille knew better. Knew him better than his wife. That made her feel a little smug about the man who was her—

What? Her almost boyfriend? Were they involved? Was being tied together through an act of violence enough to consider themselves in a relationship?

Leave it to her, to find herself connected with a man in the most bizarre way possible.

Then again, she had to consider that their relationship had started before all the trouble began. After all, they had gone out on a date.

She remembered when he asked her out. She'd been petrified and completely flustered. She'd said yes before her brain could process his question. It was as though this secret part of her brain had been waiting for the right moment to jump up and speak. In that one moment, that part of her brain—she wasn't sure if it controlled her heart or her hormones—had taken over and done the talking.

She'd spent days vacillating between canceling and going. She made up note cards on topics of conversation in case she got stuck. She practiced smiling in the mirror without too many teeth showing. And she spent a fortune on an outfit that didn't make her look too sexy.

What woman spends money on an outfit for a date to not look sexy?

Camille tossed the sponge into the sink. Opening the fridge, she took a look at the contents and decided he had the most ridiculous sweet tooth ever. Of course, it stood to reason that a man who drank mochas with extra whip cream every day would also drink grape soda. Full sugar no less.

Soda was bad for the teeth and stomach lining. The sugar levels weren't good for the metabolism and that didn't even take into account the germs on the can itself. Suddenly Camille wanted a grape soda so bad she couldn't look away from the can. She snatched it out of the fridge as if her grandfather were here and would catch her doing something sneaky. She cleaned the lid with hot water first—because she wasn't insane and cans like these were stored in warehouses where rats often nested—then popped the top and took a large gulp.

It was hideous. And wonderful.

She felt…free.

Making her way to the living room, she plopped down on his couch and let herself remember how she felt about that first date with Wyatt. For so long she blocked it, but now that seemed silly. It had happened.

She remembered that as excited, nervous and sick about that date as she had been, she'd still wanted it to go well. She wanted to flirt and laugh and have Dr. Wyatt Holladay look at her as though she was fascinating and brilliant, but not too sexy because she knew she wouldn't have been able to handle any type of advance from him.

Instead he'd questioned her belief that everything could be solved by her rigid sense of science and she'd told him he was a fruitcake.

He'd called her a condescending know-it-all.

Then she'd thrown water in his face.

She'd come home from that date and cried all night. Plus she'd done everything she could to not run into him at the hospital. Until she'd needed him.

Had she? Had she really *needed* him to review those

cases? Yes, she'd been upset by the inexplicable deaths, but she could have gone to any other surgeon in the hospital or even to the medical examiner for another review. Instead she'd sought out Wyatt.

Which led to *that* night.

Despite the confusion and ultimately the horror of realizing what had been happening in the past few days, Camille couldn't put *that* night very far from her mind. There was no blocking it. It had been, by far, the most intense sexual experience she'd ever had. Beyond that, it had been the most emotional.

Now she was here in his home and knowing that he had slept a few feet away from her last night had caused emotional upheaval. She'd clung to Aphrodite all night waiting for another intruder to break into her bedroom.

Although she was fairly certain she wanted this intruder to come find her.

He hadn't. Wyatt had been a gentleman. Damn it.

The doorbell rang and instantly, she tensed. She wasn't sure what the proper etiquette was in this situation. Did she answer it? Or pretend like no one was home.

"Camille," came a shout through the door. "I know you're in there." Delia's dulcet tones carried through the thick wood.

Seeing no other option, Camille headed for the door, but not before hiding her soda in the refrigerator first.

Approaching the small foyer, she noticed that Delia hadn't stopped banging on the door, which couldn't be a good sign. Straightening her shoulders and preparing for a fight, Camille opened it.

The woman's blouse was untucked from her skirt and her hair was a mess. She looked rattled and Camille had a suspicion as to what had caused it.

"You two couldn't leave well enough alone," she began, pushing her way past Camille into Wyatt's home.

"Someone broke into my house last night."

"So what?" Delia's hands shook as she paced Wyatt's living room. "Can't you see that the house and the car can be one thing, but those patients dying might be something else? The sheriff was in my office first thing this morning asking questions. What if this gets out? What if it makes the press? You can kiss any shot at your new surgery wing goodbye."

"Delia, you need to calm down."

"Calm down!" she shrieked. "I've worked for this hospital for years. I've built it into something special and now people are dying. Correct me if I'm wrong, but if people think there is a chance they might be murdered when they come to Physicians' Memorial the likelihood is they will stay away."

"And maybe they should until we find out what's happening. Delia, look at me." Camille waited until the older woman looked into her eyes. "I was not the cause of death for those two patients. I don't know if Chuck has had a chance to examine the third."

"Nothing," Delia muttered as she made her way to the sofa. She collapsed on it as if she'd run out of energy. "The medical examiner found nothing. No bleeds, no infection, no obvious reason for cause of death. There was a minor skin reaction around where the IV was inserted into the patient's arm, but he didn't find any drugs in her system other than what was supposed to be there. And Logan reviewed the tapes. He found…he found nothing wrong with any of the surgeries."

Because there was nothing to find. Camille had known it. Now Delia did, too. Camille sat across from her, her hands folded in her lap. "Wyatt is taking precautions."

"Wyatt," Delia said, lifting her head, "is playing hero to your damsel in distress. What must that feel like for you, the perpetual wallflower?"

"I'm not a damsel in distress," Camille snapped. "And I don't need rescuing. What I do need are some answers. My patients are dying. Someone is...obviously after me. Wants to hurt me. Right now Wyatt is the only person who seems to give a damn. You certainly don't."

Delia sighed. "I care, Camille. You're one of the most talented surgeons on the flippin' East Coast. Because of you I've been able to do what I have with this hospital. We make money. We're written up in medical journals. You are my star. Without you it all comes to a big crashing end and we go back to being a no-name suburban hospital. I don't want that."

"Then why are you fighting me on this?"

"Because it doesn't make sense," she railed. "Someone is killing patients because they're pissed off at you? Your car, totally understandable. What's the big deal to you if there is some damage to your car? Maybe even someone trying to scare you by breaking into your house, okay. But murder...in my hospital? I refuse to believe it."

"You understand why someone would key my car?" Camille slowly rose. She couldn't say why but she wanted more than a coffee table's amount of distance between her and Delia.

"Logan left because of you. You know that."

"Logan left because he couldn't handle being second best. That has to do with his ego, not mine. You know that."

Delia stood then and pointed her finger in accusation. "You rubbed it in his face! You showed him up every chance you could."

Backing up a few steps, Camille kept more than a few feet between them. "I didn't."

"You were always on call. You were always the first one any cardiology group in this area contacted when there was an emergency because they knew you would be there. Logan couldn't compete with that. He wasn't a robot like you. He had a life."

"You mean he had sex. It seems to me that must have filled all his free time given the number of partners he had."

"Don't you judge me."

Camille was fairly certain she was judging Logan, but she didn't say anything. Delia's face was red and blotchy. Her temper, something she'd been known for anyway, was out of control. Physically, the woman was taller and probably outweighed Camille by ten or twenty pounds. If she chose to act on her frustration, Camille knew she would be at a disadvantage.

There had been no cat fights with girls in her past. She'd never formed any relationships with anyone that would have necessitated fighting. She was pretty sure the most violent act she'd ever committed had been to throw water in Wyatt's face.

Water, however, was not going to calm Delia down.

"Don't you dare judge me," she repeated even as she advanced on Camille. "I was working seventy, eighty, sometimes ninety hours a week. Everything I had went into that hospital. My whole self. I needed…something for me. I needed the release. I *needed* sex with Logan. I had to have that at least. It was only fair. And you should understand that tucked away here in Wyatt's home. I see the way you look at him. Like he's ice cream and chocolate and every fantasy you've ever had about a man rolled up into one. You have to understand how I felt."

But Camille didn't understand it. She didn't need Wyatt. Not as a physical release. She didn't need him at all. Hadn't she proven that by living on her own for years without him?

But she wanted him. Wanted him very badly. It wasn't the same thing.

"I'm not judging you, Delia. I'm telling you his leaving wasn't my fault."

"His leaving ruined everything! Twice a week, sometimes three, he would come to me. I knew there were others. Hell, I knew my own damn assistant was probably next in line. But for those weeks and months he gave me something that I craved. It was like going hungry for so many years and suddenly having this feast of treats in front of you. I gorged on him and I loved it. And you took him away. He works thirty miles from here, but won't return my calls. The only reason he showed up for the debriefing is because the board asked him to, not me. No, he won't make time for those he left behind. He's got new conquests. Another CEO. More nurses. We might as well be dead to him. I'm back to being hungry again."

"So you keyed my car."

"I was angry with you that day at the hospital. The way you casually threw out to me that Logan wanted to sleep with you," Delia whispered. "So angry. First with him. When he told me he was leaving I…didn't handle it well. We fought. I tried to make him understand how good he could have it at this hospital. I would have given him every perk, every advantage I could. But all he cared about was getting as far away from you as possible. I acted out of instinct. And then you said those things…I was so angry."

Camille closed her eyes. "You need to leave."

"Aren't you listening?" Delia waved her arms and

pointed to her chest. "I did it. I trashed his car and your car and broke the windows. That was all me. Those patients dying is unrelated. You need to call off the police."

"How long did Logan stay with you yesterday after I left?" Camille wanted to know.

Delia dropped her face into her hands. "Not long enough. I wanted him so much, but he said he only wanted to be friends. As if I want a damned friend. I think he knew it was me. The car. I saw it in his face when he refused to give Wyatt names. He looked at me and he knew what I had done. I think he was disgusted with me. He left."

"You must have been angry all over again," Camille said carefully. This time she found her eyes dancing about the space, looking for a weapon. "And you had plenty of time to race to my house. Wyatt and I hadn't been in a super hurry. Maybe you had enough time to break in through the back door?"

"What are you talking about? I didn't break into your house."

"You left the noose. To scare me. Or you really intended to hurt my cat. Hard to know, isn't it?"

"You're insane," Delia muttered.

No, Camille decided. She was the only person in this room who was not insane. "Very symbolic...the noose. Considering how Logan liked to asphyxiate his lovers."

Delia's hands wrapped around her neck as if hiding the evidence of what Logan had done to her. "You don't know what he's like. You don't know how he makes a person feel."

"Cheap?"

The front door closed behind Wyatt. He stood in the foyer with his arms folded over his chest, his gaze on Delia. Camille didn't want to admit to herself how relieved she was. It made her feel like the damsel Delia accused her of being.

"I imagine he makes a person feel very cheap and disposable."

"Wyatt, you need to call off the sheriff."

"Delia, you're under the mistaken impression that I have any control over that. There are three dead bodies. The last one is being examined again by an independent medical examiner. One way or another, someone needs to find out what happened to those people."

"Fine." Delia nodded. She made an attempt to smooth her hair and tuck in her shirt. "Until the investigation is resolved, the suspension remains in place. Wyatt, I would recommend you turn over your clinic shifts to some other doctor. I can't fire you without board approval, but—"

"Already done. I'm not leaving Camille's side until whoever is behind this is caught."

"A white knight. Like I said," she spat. "The two of you stay the hell away from me."

With that she brushed past Camille and Wyatt on her way out the door, slamming it with the full force of her anger.

"You have to love that. She comes here to tell us to stay away from her."

Camille tried to smile but couldn't. "She was the one who keyed my car and Logan's, too."

"What?"

"She admitted it. I think…I think she was obsessed with Logan. Whatever he did to those people he was with made them a little crazy."

Wyatt walked over and rubbed Camille's arms, restoring warmth. Only then did she realize how cold she was. It felt good. His touch.

"Come on, let's face it. Delia always was wound a little

tight. My concern is if she was willing to go so far as to vandalize some cars, what else could she have done?"

"No, I can't believe she would have killed patients. If for no other reason than that hospital is everything to her. Damaging its reputation isn't something she would do if it would reflect badly on her."

"You have to consider that maybe she's lost the ability to rationalize. What if she thought that by ruining you, your reputation, she could lure Logan back?"

Camille couldn't accept that. She couldn't believe that Delia would be so desperate for Logan's attention that she would commit murder. Breaking a car window in anger wasn't ending the life of an innocent person.

But isn't that exactly what had been done?

For the first time the reality of what someone, likely someone she knew and worked with every day, had done came crashing down on Camille's head. *Murder.* The word was foreign to her. Almost surreal. But three people were dead and she knew that she wasn't responsible.

"How did they die, Wyatt?"

"That's what the medical examiner has to find out. But how hard could it have been? Three people, completely vulnerable after surgery. Nurses, techs, any hospital staff really, could have come and gone. Even in the ICU there's still enough traffic for a staff member to have gone unnoticed. A pillow to the face. A fifty cc syringe of air into the IV. A drug they haven't detected or more anesthesia which might not show up on the toxicology as being unusual because the medical examiner is expecting to find it after surgery. I don't know."

"I can't believe this is happening." Nothing her grandfather had taught her had prepared her for this. There was no rule for defending herself against a murderer.

Wyatt advanced on her, his face close to hers. She could

feel his intensity and in some ways it frightened her almost as much as Delia's ranting.

"Well, you need to start believing it. It is happening. Your eyes, your ears need to be open at all times. You need to be watching everything and everyone coming near you. Because I'm fairly certain that the next person this killer wants dead is you."

Chapter 12

"You cleaned the refrigerator, too."

They were standing in the kitchen together, Camille looking on while Wyatt rediscovered his home. After Delia's dramatic exit, he'd needed something to distract Camille. Commenting on her exceptional housekeeping skills was the first thing that leaped to his mind.

"It doesn't make sense to put the food you're going to be eating in an unclean environment."

Okay. Then he wouldn't tell her that he hadn't really cleaned the fridge other than a casual wipe-down since he bought the thing. He lifted the plastic lid on the side of the door. "Even the butter dish holder. Wow."

He should have worn sunglasses to protect him from the glare off all the white surfaces Camille had revealed. The countertops sparkled, the porcelain sink gleamed and he was sure that if he'd wanted to, he could have eaten off his kitchen floor.

She'd had a busy morning.

And as her reward she must have had a grape soda. He saw the open can on one of the shelves and smiled. It seemed silly but he liked that she'd felt comfortable enough to help herself. He also liked that she'd allowed herself to give in to the temptation of her sweet tooth.

Yes, Wyatt was definitely a fan of Camille giving in to any temptations she had.

"I basically cleaned everywhere except…your bedroom."

"Right. You wouldn't want to go in there." That wasn't as good a sign as the grape soda.

"I didn't want to invade your privacy."

Or she was still afraid of that aspect of their relationship and the last place she wanted to be was anywhere near his bed. He hoped he was wrong and she was telling him the truth, but he doubted it. As intense and pleasurable as that night between them had been, he felt as though he was starting all over again in terms of breaking down her walls.

"I hope you don't mind about the place," she said, obviously self-conscious. "You did give me the supplies."

"I don't. I've been concerned about the environment my food has been resting in for weeks now."

She sighed. "You're teasing me."

He was. He figured after the encounter with Delia and him sharing his belief someone wanted her dead, a little teasing was in order. He chucked her under her chin with his knuckle. "I am. I'm sorry I scared you."

"You're telling me what you think, although I don't think you're right. Whoever was in my house last night only wanted to scare me."

Or kill her cat. Which didn't need to be said.

"Do you think it was Delia?" Camille asked.

He could see she didn't want the answer to be yes. Her expression was all about bracing for pain. She didn't want to believe that the woman for whom she had worked for so many years would have gone that far for…spite, revenge? For that matter neither did Wyatt. As he'd said to Camille, he always thought Delia was wound a little tight, but killing a cat? Murdering patients in her hospital? It was too far-fetched.

But that didn't mean he wasn't going to tell the sheriff about who was responsible for the vandalism to Camille's and Logan's cars. If that put Delia on top of the suspect list, then so be it.

"I don't know. She would have had to haul ass out of that hospital to beat us to your place. Then make a noose out of some rope…I don't know."

Camille rubbed her arms. "In a way it might be worse if it wasn't her. Because that means there is someone else out there who hates me that much. I don't know if I can stand this, Wyatt."

He didn't know if he could, either. Before these spiraling events he would have considered himself a contemporary, intelligent, reasonable man. Yes, he pulled out chairs for women and opened doors because he thought it courteous, but that was as far as his old-fashioned instincts went. He thought women could be strong in many different ways. He knew plenty of them who were as capable of protecting themselves as men.

The last thing he imagined he would feel was territorial and furious about the thought of someone coming close to his woman. Hurting his woman.

But he did. Like he stepped out of the cave yesterday.

The hours he'd been apart from her while he worked his shift in the clinic had been the most stressful of his life. Some primitive instinct in him had screamed that he needed to go back from the time he left her. He needed to watch over her and protect her.

Not only had he found someone to cover his shift, he'd let several of his fellow doctors know he wasn't coming back until this was all over. Camille needed him. It made him feel as though he wanted to pound his chest and grunt a bit.

If that made him look at her as if she was his to protect, he couldn't stop it. He was, however, wise enough to keep those primitive grunts to himself. Camille probably wouldn't appreciate being thought of as his.

"Listen, we need to get your car from the hospital. No point in leaving it there and giving Delia a shot at destroying another luxury vehicle."

Wyatt waved her forward and, after a last check of the sliding glass door that led to his rear deck, and securing the lock on the front door, he felt Aphrodite was reasonably safe from intruders. As an extra precaution he'd asked his neighbor, a retired cop, to keep his eye on the place. Any hint of disturbance and he would sound the alarm. It was the best Wyatt could do.

Still, he could see Camille looking over her shoulder several times as she headed to the car, wondering if it was okay to leave.

She looked odd to him and it took him a moment to understand why. She was wearing jeans, a casual shirt and sneakers. Clothes to clean in. Her hair was pulled back into a ponytail, but instead of the slick ones she would wear at work, now tendrils escaped around her face. She looked younger than he could ever remember seeing her and he thought about what it must have taken for her to earn the respect of patients who believed she was capable of cutting into their chests.

Now someone had destroyed that. Or was trying to.

He wanted to throttle the person. He wanted to hurt Delia in some fundamental way for attacking Camille. What amazed him was that Delia wasn't the only person who felt that way. Because he couldn't…he wouldn't believe she'd kill patients out of some form of twisted revenge.

It was bad for business. And Delia was all about business.

Which meant there was a killer walking around Physicians' Memorial and everyone in that hospital was a suspect—they were likely the colleagues of a murderer. He needed to believe that. He couldn't trust anyone or let down his guard with anyone. It would be the only way to protect Camille.

She was standing by the passenger door in the reserved lot in front of his house. He watched her study the Jeep before she climbed into it. "You cleaned it. I noticed last night but I didn't say anything."

"It needed it," he said, keeping his voice casual. But of course he'd done it for her. It was a simple thing to make her feel more comfortable. He wondered how she would react if she knew that for the past few months so many of his actions were designed to bring her closer.

He knew how she'd react. She'd run in the opposite direction.

Tread lightly. It was his new mantra. She was in his house. A few feet away from where he slept. He would make her feel safe and protected and when she was ready, he would close the gap on that space and bring her back to his bed.

Wyatt wondered if this type of manipulation made him slightly evil. But then he didn't care. All's fair in love and war.

"Ready?" he asked as he started the car and pulled out of his development.

"No. I can't believe I'm going to say this but I don't think I would be sad if I never saw that hospital again."

"You're reeling from everything that's happened. When this is over—"

"It will end, right? I mean, I don't watch much television but I've seen enough crime shows to know that they always catch the bad guy. There is a dramatic scene at the end and then the bad guy, the person behind everything, is sent to jail. You have to tell me that's going to happen."

He couldn't. And she knew it. They lived in a small town in New Jersey. The last official murder in town was seven years ago, a domestic dispute that got out of hand. Now they were talking about unknown causes of death, suspicious characters and a host of suspects.

The only two common elements seemed to be Logan Dade and Camille Larson.

"We should talk to Logan," Wyatt announced. He pulled the Jeep over next to a sidewalk and put it into Park.

"Why?"

"Well, if I'm right and someone is killing those patients as a way to target you, then we agree the reason seems to be the role you played in Logan's departure. We know Delia was sleeping with him."

"And Marie."

"Delia keyed your car and Logan's. Maybe Marie took his departure a little harder than that."

"You think Marie could have…"

"I'm speculating," Wyatt said. He didn't want to think a nurse might be capable of murder and he didn't want to color his judgment of her with crazy ideas. However, a nurse would know any number of ways to kill a patient without leaving a mark and would be the last person to arouse suspicion in a hospital. Wyatt tried not to think about that.

"Ultimately, it's up to the police to build a case. But someone came after you last night. If I'm right, maybe the same person also tried to run you off the road. That speaks to a violent temper. If we could talk to Logan alone, without Delia and a room full of doctors, he might be more willing to name names. We would know who to be cautious of at the very least. It's a good idea."

"Are you trying to convince me or yourself?"

"Both of us. I'm not a detective. I solve medical puzzles not criminal ones, but arming ourselves with knowledge can't be a bad idea."

"Okay. But it's Sunday. I doubt he'll be at the hospital. Do you know where he lives?"

"Yeah, he hosted a poker night once for a bunch of the doctors."

"I don't remember anything like that."

Wyatt laughed. "That's because it was for men only. Logan made a big to-do of smoking cigars and hiring this girl dressed as a maid to serve us drinks. Said it was important for men to spend time with men. That women weakened us. I thought it was pathetic. It was my first and last poker night."

With that, he waited for traffic to clear then made a U-turn. He took a quick glance in the rearview mirror to make sure a patrolman hadn't seen his illegal move, but spotted only a black car behind a few car lengths back.

"Maybe after being with Delia he did feel that way. She was so intense about him...well, I could see how it could be draining."

"Real relationships aren't like that." Wyatt needed her to know that. "Real relationships are about give and take. Anything that one-sided is bound to be destructive."

"I know," she said quietly. "I mean I don't *know* how it all works but I can imagine that's how it's supposed to be. Do you know there was a moment when Delia was ranting and flailing about, I actually felt fear? She was out of control. It was how I knew she'd been the one to key my car. Someone that angry had to have acted on it. I thought…I thought…"

"You thought she could have killed someone," he said, finishing the sentence she didn't want to finish.

"It's inconceivable." Camille shook her head. "I've worked for the woman for years. She runs a profitable hospital. She's intelligent, hardworking—"

"And she had no life outside of work, no real relationships that I ever recall because, like I said, what she had with Logan wasn't real. And not that many friends, if her treatment of you is any indication," Wyatt enumerated.

"Gee, now that I think about it, it sounds like someone else I know." Out of the corner of his eye he caught her scrunched face. "She could have snapped. That's all I'm saying."

"Is that what you think might happen to me? That I might snap?"

Wyatt sighed. "I sure would like to see you bend a little before that happened. Talk to me, Camille. Tell me why you work so hard to keep people away. Why won't you let anyone into your life?"

"There is no time…I'm focused on my work," she said tightly.

"*I'm* focused on my work. You are obsessed with it. You mentioned your grandfather the other night. You said he raised you. What was he like?" Wyatt could feel the tension build next to him and for a moment he thought she wouldn't respond.

"I didn't tell you who he was."

"I know he was a doctor. You said he mentored you. Would I know his name?"

"Yes. My grandfather was Dr. Conrad Slazenger."

Wyatt blinked a few times. "*The* Slazenger? The actual Slazenger? The man was a pioneer. A revolutionary, a—"

"My grandfather. Larson was my mother's name. My parents never married."

"I see." And Wyatt did see. Those were some pretty big shoes to fill. "He was stern, I take it."

"He was driven. He was ambitious and he wanted me to be the same. I *am* the same. I haven't gotten to where I am solely because he pushed me here. I had to want it for myself. But Grandfather didn't see a need for things like school and friends and play dates and all the rest. He isolated me so that I could keep my focus."

Wyatt snorted. "He isolated you so that he could keep you all to himself."

"You're wrong."

"I'm not. You told me that your father didn't follow in your grandfather's footsteps. And after you were dumped in his lap he couldn't handle the responsibility and took off. You don't mention a grandmother—"

"She died years before I was born."

"There you have it. Your grandfather had already lost his wife, he essentially lost his son and then you show up and he's got another chance. So he gripped you tight and didn't let go because he was afraid of losing you."

"That's psychobabble. You sound like Dr. Rosen."

"That's fact. Unfortunately, what your Dr. Frankenstein grandfather didn't realize as he was molding you into the perfect surgeon is that he was depriving you of the things you needed to have a normal life."

It was a hard thing for Wyatt. Slazenger was one of the people he wished he'd had one hour with to talk medicine before the man died. But thinking of Camille as a little girl with scary dreams and no one to turn to and no friends to play with made him want to read the old man the riot act as well.

"Normal," she repeated. "I really did want...normal. That must sound boring to you."

"No, it sounds about right. Normal is friends and family. Normal is work, sure, but it's also play. Normal is good sex and good times and laughter. You can have that, Camille."

This time she snorted. "Yeah right. After all these years—"

"You can't get back what you lost," he stopped her. "But you can choose to live differently going forward."

"Says the man who wants me to have sex with him."

"Hell, yeah." Wyatt didn't say another word. He let Camille sit with her thoughts as he drove over the bridge into Philadelphia.

Unlike Camille and himself, Logan had chosen city life over suburbia. He had a downtown penthouse that overlooked William Penn that was filled with leather, glass and chrome. He called it his fortress of solitude as he never brought any of his lovers there.

Logan didn't like to share his life. During poker he'd joked with the other doctors that his motto was simple: get in and get out. In a way, Wyatt had felt sorry for him. If he didn't change his attitude, then he was going to spend the rest of his life without any meaningful relationships.

Of course, then he'd made a crude joke about the girl who was serving the drinks and Wyatt had wanted to deck him.

He circled the block a few times and got lucky as a car pulled away from the curb. Together they made their way to the lobby and asked the concierge to call Logan and let him know he had visitors.

"Do you think he'll see us?" Camille whispered.

"I can't imagine why he wouldn't. He probably wants this thing done as much as we do."

"Dr. Dade will see you," the concierge announced.

They rode the elevator to the top floor and made their way to his door. Wyatt knocked and wasn't all that surprised to find Logan answering the door in nothing more than a silk robe. Logan also believed in the fewer clothes the better. Hell, Wyatt figured they were lucky he didn't answer the door buck naked.

"Doctors," Logan said. "What a surprise. To what do I owe this honor? Because I'm fairly certain you two didn't come here for a threesome."

"Yeah," Wyatt drawled. "You can be fairly certain of that."

Behind him he could practically hear Camille gagging. His girl had good taste.

"I want answers, Logan."

"Well, then," he said, opening his door to let them inside. "You had better start with the questions."

Chapter 13

Camille did everything she could to avoid looking at the gap in Logan's robe. He was sitting on his couch, a drink in his hand with his legs sprawled wide. She knew he'd done it intentionally as if to show off what she'd missed. She had to suppress the urge to let him know that Wyatt was much more…impressive…in that department. But she didn't imagine that would help them with the answers they were looking to get from him.

"How many people were you seeing, Dade?" Wyatt started with.

"What makes you think I'm going to discuss my love life with you?"

"Because people are dying."

"That has nothing to do with me." Logan stood, the silk material flapping around him. He went to his wet bar and dropped more ice cubes in his glass. Camille watched him pour dark liquor over the cubes and wondered how many drinks he'd had before they got there. It was only five o'clock and he was already two down. Maybe what was happening at his old job was bothering him more than he let on.

"It has everything to do with you," Wyatt said.

"You don't know that. And if coming here to accuse me of murder is your idea of spending a fine Sunday afternoon, then you can leave."

Wyatt leaned back in his chair. "Look, I know you didn't have a hand in their deaths. You can't be held responsible. But still, people are dying."

"Yeah, well, maybe I better take another look at the videos. I mean, I told Delia I didn't see anything, but maybe a second pass would help point the finger at your incompetence."

"Logan, don't," Camille said quietly. She looked at him and waited for him to meet her eyes. "Don't lie about that. Lie about why you left or that we were involved. Lie about anything else. But you and I together have replaced hearts. You've seen me operate. You didn't need those tapes to know what happened in the OR. And as much as you hate me, I know you respect me. I did not kill those people on the table."

Logan closed his eyes. "Fine. Conceded. So, you're saying that someone murdered patients because I dumped her. I've dumped a lot of people over the years, Camille. Nobody has ever resorted to murder before."

"How many people have keyed your car?" Wyatt wondered.

"I know who was responsible for that. And trust me, that person did not kill patients." Logan took a sip of his drink. "It would be bad for business."

"We know it was Delia," Camille said. "She admitted it to me."

"There, you see? It was Delia. I went in to give her my two weeks. She flipped out. Said she couldn't handle the thought of losing me. The next day my car is trashed. It was extreme, yes, but it's not the first time someone wasn't ready to let go. But you and I agree she wouldn't have killed anyone. Which means the stuff with the cars is totally unrelated."

"Maybe, unless you want to tell us who else you were seeing who didn't want to let go."

Logan pursed his lips and shook his head. "I told you, I'm not naming names. It's bad enough what's happened to Delia."

"Bad enough? She might be a murderer." Wyatt stood and shoved his hands into his pockets. "As much as I hate to think she could have done it, given her actions I'm sure the sheriff is going to take a long, hard look at her. But I want to be prepared if it's not her. Which means I need names."

"If you want the names of everyone I've slept with in the past month, we're going to be here awhile."

Camille could see Wyatt clench his jaw in irritation.

"Fine. How about the ones with a temper? The ones who didn't want to let go when you were done with them. We know you were seeing Marie—"

"I was seeing a lot of nurses."

"Names, Logan. I need names."

He paused for a moment as if thinking, but shook his head. "No. No one kills for sex. You're going down the wrong path."

Now it was Camille's turn to hide her irritation. He was lying. She could see it. Either he didn't want to confess that he might know the person responsible or he truly didn't want to believe it. Camille glanced around the open space and wondered if the view from the top floor was going to be enough to assuage his conscience if someone else got hurt.

There was a counter that separated the living space from the kitchen beyond. A blinking light caught Camille's attention. It was the dock for a portable phone. The hand set wasn't in it but the blinking light on the base reminded her what her own phone did when she had messages.

"Is someone calling you, Logan? Leaving messages you don't want to hear?" Camille pointed to the phone.

"I didn't want to be disturbed," he answered easily.

"I wonder," Wyatt said as he looked out through the massive glass windows that showcased the city below. "If we were to listen, how many messages would there be? And how many would be from the same person?"

"I'm sure some would be from Delia. She's using Camille's suspension as an excuse to contact me. You know, I would say it was all rather flattering if I didn't think part of Delia's reason for being so pissed was that she lost a surgeon. Not a lover."

Wyatt faced him then. "And she's really the only one. The only one who might have gone off the deep end to do something this extreme."

Logan took another sip of his drink.

A buzzing sound echoed in the room and caught their attention. It sounded like it was coming from the table in the foyer. Camille recognized the sound instantly.

"Shit. That's my buzzer. I'm on call." Logan set his drink on the bar and went to go fetch it. He picked it up and cursed. "I need a second." He headed down the hallway to what Camille imagined was his bedroom.

"Obviously he doesn't have the issues with drinking on call you do," Wyatt muttered once Logan was out of sight.

"He's lying," Camille whispered. "I can see when

you're asking him these questions that there is a person he's thinking of. Why doesn't he tell us?"

"I don't know. Maybe he really doesn't want to believe anyone he was with is actually dangerous."

Wyatt's attention was caught by the entertainment unit he was pacing in front of. He stopped and knelt down. Then hit a button on the CD player.

"What are you doing? Now is not the time to be checking out the electronics."

"I noticed it was on. I wonder if he was watching your surgeries before we came up. Maybe one last time to spot something unusual."

Camille didn't see the relevance. "More likely it's some tasteless movie only men enjoy. If you pull that out and the title is some horrible porn name, I don't want to know it."

Wyatt held the CD around his finger. His face was tight, his expression was unreadable. "Not a porn name. Your name."

"What?"

Wyatt put the CD back in the machine. He looked for and found the remote on the coffee table. As he turned on the TV, Camille thought he'd lost his mind and was about to tell him so when images of her filled the screen.

This wasn't her in the middle of a surgery.

"What the hell are you doing?" Logan shouted as he came back in the room. He lunged for Wyatt, but Wyatt easily sidestepped him. His eyes never left the screen.

Camille couldn't move. She was frozen in place as she watched herself. She was removing her clothes in the locker room. Tucked away in the corner she knew so well, but somewhere above her there must have been a camera in one of the lockers. She watched as she stripped out of her scrubs left only in her serviceable bra and panties.

Then the scene switched and she was in the shower.

In the shower, naked and completely unaware of the camera that was mounted somewhere on the wall.

The scene shifted again, only this time it was Camille in surgery. It was a tape of a transplant she had Logan had performed together. They were standing side by side discussing their plan of attack.

Why? Why would he intersperse pictures of her in the shower with images of them in surgery together. It made no sense.

"Turn it the hell off!" Logan roared. This time he made another lunge for Wyatt and pulled the remote out of his hand. While Logan worked frantically to turn off the TV, he didn't see Wyatt turn back toward him.

"You sick..." Wyatt didn't finish his thought with words. The sound of flesh hitting flesh wasn't pleasant. The crack registered and Camille could see Logan hit the ground, his hand flying to his nose.

"You bastard," Logan mumbled even as the blood poured through his fingers. "You broke it."

"Damn it!" Wyatt clutched his fist with his hand, wincing in obvious pain. "Man, that hurts."

"That's why hitting is not advisable for a doctor. We typically seek to avoid pain," Camille chastised.

Unable to watch anyone bleed needlessly, she stepped over Logan and made her way to the kitchen where she grabbed a bunch of towels. She handed them to him and watched as he applied pressure to stop the bleeding.

"Why?" Camille asked, crouching so that she was eye level with him.

"Don't let him answer. He was taping you. Filming you. Freaking cameras in the lockers and the showers. I should have your perverted ass thrown in jail."

Logan shook his head. "Get out. Both of you get out."

The words were mumbled through the towels now soaked with blood.

"But the surgeries. You edited film of me getting undressed with us operating…" Camille understood she wasn't sexually sophisticated. But this seemed…strange.

Logan shrugged one shoulder. "It's where I did my best work. Always. With you. But you never saw me, did you? Never once. Why didn't you ever see me? I had everyone I wanted. All I needed to do was crook my finger. But never with you."

"I—" Camille didn't know what to say. She wouldn't say she was sorry. Not for refusing to be another notch on his belt.

"You going to tell us what we need to know?" Wyatt asked one more time.

"I. Don't. Know. Anything." It was said as clearly as it could be with a broken nose.

"Let's go."

Camille could feel Wyatt grabbing her arm, but she resisted the tug. She wanted answers. None of this made any sense to her.

They were to the elevators before her thoughts stopped reeling enough to address what happened. "I don't understand."

"What's not to understand?" Wyatt asked angrily. "The man was secretly videotaping you."

"Wyatt," she said, reaching for his arm.

He took a long breath. Then another one. "I'm going back there and killing him."

Fortunately the elevator doors opened and Camille could steer him inside before that happened. She hit the lobby button.

"I knew he was…perverted. But…"

"He was watching the damn CD before we got there. Probably… Damn it!"

Camille was grateful Wyatt didn't try to finish that sentence. "I understand all that but why add in video of me operating? Am I missing something? Some blood fetish? Because if that's the case, then that man seriously needs to be analyzed before he's allowed back in an operating room."

"Don't you get it?"

Wyatt was looking at her with a confused expression on his face, as if he couldn't understand how she didn't know what he apparently knew. She felt foolish. Like everyone was in on the joke except her.

"Get what?"

The doors opened to the lobby. Camille hurried out before getting her answer. Suddenly she didn't want Wyatt to say any more. It was enough that she was dealing with the concept that someone—maybe her boss—was a killer. That was certainly enough to handle in one day.

"Camille, hold up!"

She didn't wait, simply kept heading out the doors and onto the sidewalk.

Wyatt jogged up behind her. "Running from me isn't going to make it go away."

"I wasn't running away from you, I was running away from…" All the things she didn't want to know.

It was after six o'clock and the sun was starting to set on the city. A Sunday night, the streets were nearly empty. Camille could see across the street to where Wyatt had parked and she desperately wanted to go there. Get in and drive away and never look back.

"Don't you see, it makes even more sense now."

"Stop talking as if I understand what you mean. None of this is logical!"

Wyatt held her arms and waited for her to meet his eyes. "He's in love with you. Or the closest thing he can come to it. Infatuation, obsession."

"What? That's beyond crazy."

"No, only crazy in your mind because you can't imagine how anyone could be. That's going to be a problem, Camille. One you need to get over."

"Logan is a narcissistic, egocentric, arrogant ass. He loves his penis and himself in that order."

"I agree you might take a distant third, but it's there. That's why the video of you in surgery. You weren't alone, Camille. You were with him. As a team. That meant something to him."

"He can't be."

"Why?"

There was a bite in his words and she instinctively wanted to retreat, but his grip on her shoulders wouldn't allow her.

"Why can't he love you? You're beautiful—"

"I'm not. I'm plain—"

"You're beautiful and smart and talented," he said, talking over her. "You don't play games with people because you don't know how. You care about the people you operate on rather than treating them like slabs of meat. You have everything in you to give, everything that has been storing up inside of you for years because you thought you weren't worthy or you were too scared to give it to anyone. Logan saw that. I see that."

The words were being fired at her but she didn't hear them. Or wouldn't hear them. She wasn't sure.

Wyatt shook his head and then looked into her eyes. "I love you, Camille. God, I do. I think I have for so long."

"No." She couldn't handle love. She could barely handle sex. She broke away from him and found herself once again looking to his Jeep. Looking for escape. She stepped onto the road and saw no traffic. It wasn't until she was halfway across the street that she heard it…the roar of a car getting closer.

Turning to her left, she saw a dark car with tinted windows, windows like the car that had nearly run her off the road. It was barreling down on her fast. Instinct had her turning and jumping out of the way.

The car missed her by no more than inches. She felt the heat of the engine as it sped by.

"Camille!"

Wyatt sprinted to reach her. He grabbed her hand and hauled her off the pavement. Her hands were scraped and she'd banged her knee, but none of the pain compared to the fear as she saw the car make a U-turn in the middle of the road.

It was coming back for them.

Wyatt tried pulling her toward the building but the driver didn't seem to have a problem crossing onto the wrong side of the road. The car cut them off from the building door, the engine roaring as it turned to come after them again.

"Run!"

Wyatt grabbed Camille's wrist and dragged her along with him down the street in the opposite direction. She couldn't fathom what this person was attempting to do. Scare her, hit her or toy with her. She ran as fast as she could to keep up with Wyatt, who was turning the corner of the city block.

A mailbox bolted to the sidewalk slowed the menacing black car as it made the sharp turn. For a heartbeat they were out of sight around the corner of the building.

"Is there a side door?" she puffed out.

"No."

Across the street shops were closed with gated windows

and barred doors. No place to find shelter. Behind them the roar of the engine grew louder. They couldn't outrun it and there was no place to hide.

"There! There might be…" Wyatt pointed, but didn't wait for Camille to see where he was pointing. Instead he yanked her hand, running with her down the block until it opened into a smaller alley between two buildings. She didn't know what he was thinking. The alley wasn't so small that the car wouldn't be able to follow them. She could see it ran all the way through to the next block, cut off only by a Dumpster situated halfway down. She and Wyatt hurried along either side looking for a door to one of the buildings. The first one Wyatt reached was locked.

She started to run past him, searching for another side door. The sound of the engine rumbling into the alley sent another bolt of panic straight into her heart. It revved once, then again, almost like the person was playing a game with them.

She watched it, walking backwards and stumbling, but unable to take her eyes off the threatening machine. It was as if the car itself was stalking her, not the driver behind the wheel. Beyond the tinted windshield, Camille could see nothing.

"Who are you?" she screamed as the engine roared again. And then because she couldn't help it she whispered, "Delia?"

The sound of squealing tires reached her before she could register that the car was moving again.

"Camille!"

She turned her head at the sound of his voice. Wyatt grabbed her hand and pulled her after him. Then he lifted her and she realized his intent.

The Dumpster.

She fell into the garbage with a plop then moved to give

Wyatt room. He jumped in behind her and reached for her, wrapping her in his arms.

"Hold on."

Camille wasn't sure what he wanted her to hold on to as she was the one being held. But then she felt the impact of metal on metal and knew the car had crashed into them. She felt the impact throughout her body, but the Dumpster maintained its integrity. They spun around and then stopped.

"Whoever it is will have to get out of the car to come get us," Wyatt whispered in her hair.

"What if they're armed?"

"If you've got a gun, I'm not sure why you would use a car to try and kill someone. Much less efficient."

But the point was moot as the sound of the car driving away and out of the alley was unmistakable.

Wyatt made as if to stand and check out the scene, but Camille grabbed his arm. "No. Wait! Wait until it's really gone."

He resisted her tug and stood anyway, lifting himself over the metal side. "It's really gone. Come on, we're reporting this to the police."

She nodded. The police. They would ask for the make and the model of the vehicle but all she would be able to tell them was black. Black car and tinted windows. Hopefully, Wyatt would be able to tell them more.

Camille tried to push off whatever was underneath her to get the momentum to stand. And that's when she saw it. An empty honey jar. A trash bag spilling open with crumpled napkins falling out of the bag's mouth. A lid. Cans. Lots of cans. A wilted head of lettuce. A large wad of tissues…

She was in trash. She was lying in someone else's trash. And it was so dirty….

She screamed then. Loud and long. She didn't stop screaming even when Wyatt pulled her out of the garbage. She screamed until she couldn't think or see or hear. And she didn't think she would ever stop.

Chapter 14

Eventually, the screaming did stop once they crossed the Ben Franklin Bridge into New Jersey. But what followed was worse.

"Talk to me, Camille."

Instead she rocked in the passenger seat, her eyes forward, her mind completely shut down. Wyatt had seen patients in mental facilities in better condition. She was nearly catatonic.

Getting her out of the garbage and into his Jeep had been one of the most nerve-racking experiences of his life. Forget having almost been run down by a psychopath with a thing for Chevys. The screaming drove a knife through his heart. No words had helped. He'd been unable to reach through the phobia and the gut-wrenching disgust he knew she was feeling.

Medical pioneer or not, her grandfather was a complete asshole for doing this to her.

Now Wyatt felt as though she was slipping away from him, as though he was losing her to the fear.

"You need to stay with me. Okay. I don't want to have to take you to see Dr. Rosen."

He knew that might jar her. She hated that everyone knew she'd seen a psychiatrist. But Physicians' Memorial wasn't a place where you could hide that detail, despite the laws designed to protect people from exposure. He remembered thinking at the time that Rosen wasn't going to help her. It would have required her to open up and trust the man. Wyatt was coming to understand how difficult that was for her.

"That's the last thing you want," he continued, feeling as though he was alone in the conversation. "He'll want to analyze you. Figure out your childhood trauma. Tell you to blame your mother. Or, in your case, your grandfather. But there is nothing wrong with you, Camille. Nothing wrong."

He saw her flinch at that. The rocking stopped abruptly.

"Everything is wrong with me," she said in a tight whisper.

He was so happy she was communicating, he didn't want her to stop. Even if what she said made him want to shout at her. "No, you're scared of things. Lots of people are scared of things. I was scared of chest cutters. You're scared of trash. There is nothing wrong with that, Camille. Nothing."

"I'm contaminated," she sobbed. "The germs—"

"Don't think about it. Think about the shower. Okay. We're only a few minutes away now. Think about hot water. Soap. Suds. Think about how good that's going to feel. Only that."

Wyatt waited for her response, hoping she was still with

him. Then it came. A soft *okay* that barely made it past her lips.

From then on he became a man with a mission. NASCAR driver Jimmie Johnson had nothing on him when it came to speed and control. He had no thought other than to get her home and in the shower. A small part of his brain said he should have called the sheriff on his cell. But he knew if he did, the sheriff would have met them at his place. There would be questions to answer, descriptions of the vehicle to give as well as a timeline of the event. He needed to get Camille clean before any of that could happen. And he wanted to make sure she was back from the dark place she was in right now before anyone saw her.

When all of this was over she would go back to being a surgeon and her reputation would once again need to be spotless. Nobody needed to know that she couldn't handle a trip into a Dumpster. Even a rumor that she had insecurities or periods of instability could hurt her. He wouldn't allow that.

The police would wait. The car was gone. And he couldn't see what difference an hour or two would make. In this moment, Camille came first.

Finally he pulled up to his town house. He barely had the key out of the ignition before he was jumping out of his seat and racing over to the passenger's side.

Her hands were unsteady and she was fumbling to get the door open. He did it for her and she nearly fell on top of him.

"Get away from me." She tried to push him back but she could barely stand, her muscles locked in place from how tightly she'd been holding herself. She moved stiffly and slowly.

"Get over it." He picked her up in his arms and raced to his door. Setting her down, he unlocked the door. Aphrodite greeted them, but quickly sensed her presence wasn't needed and she scurried off to hide.

"Shower, now."

Camille started to move but it was as if she'd aged a hundred years in the last hour and each step was an effort. He watched her literally push one foot in front of the other. Wyatt grabbed a trash bag out of the closet and then scooped her up around her waist to move her more quickly down the hallway.

"No, don't touch me. I'm covered in filth."

He didn't bother to argue, simply stepped into the bathroom and immediately turned on the water in the shower. Blasting it to hot, steam filled the room. He wanted her to see that. He wanted her to know how hot that water was going to be so that it would kill every germ she could imagine.

He raised her hands above her head and pulled off her T-shirt. Like a little girl, she stood still and didn't fight him. Then came her bra, her jeans, panties, socks and sneakers. All of it went into the trash bag. He did the same, dumping his clothes into the bag with no thought of trying to salvage them. She needed to see that they would be destroyed. Not washed and dried, but completely gone.

Leaning into the stall, he turned down the heat until it was still scorching hot, but bearable to the touch.

"In you go." With a push he sent her into the walk-in shower and positioned her directly under the spray. But it wasn't until he put the bar of soap in her hands, that she came out of her immobile state.

As if he'd flipped on some switch in her, she went to work scrubbing. Arms, legs, hands, feet. It was like nothing he'd ever seen. As hard as she was scrubbing, she could have taken a couple of layers off her skin. But he had to let her do it. She had to know for herself that she was once again clean.

Wyatt stepped into the shower with her and waited until she slowed down, grateful for a large hot water tank.

"You done?"

She was scrubbing her hands again with the soap, rinsing them only to scrub and rinse them again. And again. And again.

"That's it, Camille. They're clean."

She popped her head up at him and he could see that she just realized she was in the shower with him.

"I need to get clean, too," he said brushing his finger along her steamy red cheek.

He could see the effort she made and knew she was struggling against some inner instinct, but eventually she handed over the bar of soap.

She was going to be all right. In that moment he was sure of it. She was stronger than her fears.

Wyatt scrubbed himself as thoroughly if not as violently. The whole time Camille watched him, not in any sexual way, but more clinically. As if she was inspecting his approach to cleanliness and assuring herself that he hadn't missed any spots. By the time he set the bar of soap in the dish the water was starting to cool down.

He nudged her out of the stall and found a towel in his cabinet for her. Wrapping her in it, he pushed her to sit on the lid of the toilet while he grabbed another towel for himself.

Dry, he kneeled in front of her. She pulled the edges of the towel closer. Her hair was wet and loose around her shoulders, her face was the color of a strawberry, and her shoulders were up around her ears. She looked like she was five years old. It would have been adorable if it hadn't been instigated by such awful circumstances.

"You feel better?"

She nodded.

He wanted her to speak. He wanted her to say something that assured him she was better. "You going to be all right?"

Again, a nod. He needed to ask something that wasn't a yes or no question.

"I'm going to make us some dinner. What do you want to eat?"

Her eyes drifted off, and for a second she shuddered. "Not spaghetti."

He laughed, remembering the stuff had been sticking to their clothes. Yeah, his girl really was going to be okay. "You got it. No spaghetti."

She reached a hand out from the towel encompassing her and touched the side of his cheek. Other than when they had made love her touches were so rare. So precious. He froze, not wanting to give her any reason to break the contact.

"You must think I'm crazy."

"You know I don't."

Camille smiled then. "Maybe that's because you're crazy."

Wyatt considered that. "Not impossible."

"You saved us."

He couldn't stop his jaw from clenching. He knew she felt the muscle tense, but she didn't take her hand away. The thought of what could have happened to her made the anger return in a large wave. When he found the person responsible for this, he was going to kill him. Hippocratic Oath be damned.

But still she was touching him. Her hand drifting from his face to his shoulder. "I feel like my world has been turned upside down in the course of a few days."

"It has. But not everything has been awful. You're here with me."

"I'm here with you," she whispered. "Please make me forget for a little while. I don't want to think about anything. I don't want to be afraid anymore. I don't…"

"What *do* you want?"

Her eyes, so vulnerable, met his directly. "You."

His heart thudded in his chest and he wondered if he was ever going to understand what it was about Camille Larson that made it beat this way. Then again, he didn't have to question it if he didn't want to. He could feel it. And that was enough.

Standing in front of her, he flicked the towel off his waist. He was growing hard in front of her eyes and experienced an erotic bolt of pleasure as she watched it happen. Her hand reached for him and he closed his eyes and concentrated on how good it felt.

"Come on, baby. Let's go to bed."

He removed her hand with a silent promise to himself that as soon as they were lying down again he would let her have her way with him. The towel fell from her shoulders as she stood. In a rush of masculine satisfaction at having his woman with him, naked, he lifted her off her feet and into his arms.

She buried her face against his neck as he carried her to his bedroom and he could feel her sucking at the skin there, her teeth nipping at his earlobe.

"I feel different," she said between love bites. "I feel all this crazy energy. I feel like I could…devour you."

The physician in him knew that she'd experienced a shock. That what she was feeling was, in fact, an increase in her adrenaline levels. The man, however, wanted to be devoured.

He knew that often sex could be about power. Camille

had lost all of hers. By being suspended, her home broken into, her life being videotaped by an obsessed doctor. Now it was time to give her some of her power back.

Setting her on her feet beside the bed, Wyatt stripped off the covers. Then he lay down on his back, his hands beneath his head, his sex pointing straight up as a testament to his feelings on being consumed.

"You want me. Take me."

He watched her blink slowly a few times.

"I took you the last time. Each time. Now it's your turn. Take what you want, Camille. You're completely in control."

He could see her react to the word *control* and knew that she understood what he was offering. She smiled and once again reached to touch his erection. No dilly-dallying for his girl. No soft touches of his nipples or maybe a brush of her hand against his stomach. Nope, she wanted the whole enchilada upfront and he loved that about her.

"That's it. A little harder."

She climbed on the bed then, between his legs. He spread them a little wider for her so she could touch his balls if she wanted that, too. Anything she wanted, whatever she needed. All of it would be hers. He would lie still if it killed him. Sure, it would be a sacrifice, he thought. But a man had to do what he could for the woman he loved. Right now she needed him to be a feast.

His eyes narrowed to slits as he felt bolts of pleasure running up and down his body. However, he managed to keep them open enough that he could watch her exploration. Watch her face when she slid her hand around the head of his erection. Watch her reaction when he couldn't hold back a groan and she knew what she'd done had been especially pleasing.

He wanted to tell her to squeeze his shaft harder. He

wanted to tell her to play with his balls. He wanted to tell her he needed her mouth. Craved it like a starving man craves food, but this wasn't his show, it was hers. So he bit his tongue and let her stroke her fingers up and down. At one point she shifted her weight on her knees and he could see her breasts sway gently with the movement. This time he had to close his eyes or he wouldn't have been able to keep his hands to himself. He wanted to feel her tight little nipples in his palms, then in his mouth.

Later, he promised himself. Later when it would be his turn.

"I've never…"

He opened his eyes and saw that her mouth was poised over his erection. He inhaled sharply, then calmly let out his breath. "You don't have to do anything you're not comfortable with. I only want what you want."

"I didn't think I would ever be able…I had such a hard time with kissing at first."

"I love the way you kiss me," he told her. That reminded him that he needed her kisses, too. His tongue in her mouth, hers in his.

Later.

"I want to try."

Oh goodness. Keep it together. "Whatever you want, baby. I'm all yours…ah." An explosion of sensation hit as she took the head into her mouth. But it was enough. It was more than enough.

She pulled back and smiled at him. "How was that? I think I liked it, the feel of it. How did I do?"

"You did it really, really good."

"I think you mean well," she said as she bent over and again put her mouth to him.

Grammar. She wanted him to have correct grammar? She should be grateful he could grunt let alone speak.

Because now she was doing something with her tongue and it was driving him insane. He couldn't stop himself from lifting his hips, trying to sink more deeply into the wet softness of her mouth.

"Okay, stop." Wyatt sat up a bit and put his hand on her shoulder, but she seemed far too into her task. "Please, Camille, stop. I don't want to come." And he wouldn't, not in her mouth. For one, she wasn't ready for that kind of intimacy and for another he wanted to be deep inside her body when he did. Nothing had ever felt as good as coming inside of Camille.

She lifted her head and lowered her eyes almost as if she was ashamed for having enjoyed it as much as she did.

"Don't worry," he teased. "I'll let you do that again. Heck, every day if you want."

She chuckled then and the soft noise made him feel good. The trauma of nearly being run down was gone from her consciousness. He knew he wouldn't be able to hold it at bay indefinitely, but for now they were enjoying each other. Laughing. Feeling good. This, he could give her and it made him feel like a king to do so.

"But now I need you a little closer."

"Closer?"

"Hmm," he said lying down again, leaving his hands free this time to cup her breasts. There were her nipples. Nice and tight in his palms the way he wanted. "Yeah, a little farther."

Getting the idea, she straddled his hips. The soft hair covering her sex brushed his erection in a way that had him twisting his hips for more contact. "Is this close enough?"

She was teasing him. Great almighty, she was rubbing herself against his sex, wetting it with her own excitement and teasing him in the process. If he hadn't loved her already, he would have loved her in that moment.

"Nope. Not close enough."

She held him in place with her hand while she positioned her body over him, letting him press inside. "What about now?"

"Closer," he squealed like a girl. And then she did it. Sinking down, she took him fully inside her body in one long, slow ride. He heard her gasp, felt her move her hips around to get better situated, and then she sighed with what he hoped was satisfaction.

"Better?"

"The best," he murmured, pushing up in slow thrusts. Her hands fell to his chest to help her keep her balance. He remembered that this was supposed to be her show, and if he were really kind he would let her control the ride.

But a man only had so much kindness in him and what she'd done to him with her mouth had taken him too far down the path to let her enjoy an easy pace. Gripping her hips, he held her steady while he pumped into her.

Confident she had the rhythm down, he freed her right hip to trail his hand up to her breasts. He could feel them and see them bouncing with each of his thrusts and it was erotic as hell. Then he let his hand drift down her body, over her pale belly into her nest of curls. Setting a knuckle right on the spot where she needed him, so that each time he moved within her his knuckle stroked.

Four or maybe five strokes into it he felt her squeeze her body all around him and a wash of red color ran up her breasts and neck and cheeks. He wanted her to scream. Wanted to hear his name being shouted out, declaring that he was the one who had given her ecstasy. But instead she held it all inside, her body jerking a little with convulsions.

Another thrust and he was with her. Holding himself deep inside her, feeling his seed spurting out into her. He wanted to make her pregnant. Knew it was impossible with her on the pill, but still he wanted it.

She fell onto his chest, her face pressed into his neck where she placed gentle kisses. He wrapped his arms around her and thought about what they might have together once all this was behind them.

True love. Each other. Kids. A family. He needed to convince her it was possible. He needed her to know there could be more to a family than abandonment and grooming.

What he really needed was for her to love him.

Chapter 15

"Is this wrong?"

Wyatt took his eyes off the slice of pizza he was about to bite into. Camille was already chewing a sizeable mouthful of dough, sauce, cheese, sausage, meatball and pepperoni. It had taken him a few minutes to convince her that pepperoni was essential to a real meat pizza, but eventually he wore her down.

Now she was sitting crossed-legged wearing one of his T-shirts and he was in a pair of sweatpants—only because he had to open the door to the delivery person. They were still in bed eating meat pizza after amazing sex. It was his dream come true.

"What could be wrong about this?"

"We should have called the police. We need to give them a description of the car. I'm certain it is the same one that passed me the other day on the way to your house."

"Yeah, I figured. Strange thing, too, is I think I've seen

it before. The tinted windshield isn't something you see a lot."

"After we eat?"

Wyatt looked at the clock. It was going on eleven at night. It was Sunday. "If we call now we'll get some shift worker. I say we wait and head to the station tomorrow morning. We'll speak with the sheriff directly. There is nothing anyone can do right now."

"So we're going to eat pizza and go to sleep?"

At that moment Aphrodite chose to join them, hopping up on the bed to inspect the box. Wyatt lopped off a piece of meatball and dropped it in front of her.

"Don't give her any pepperoni," Camille warned.

"Why?" The cat seemed pretty happy with the meatball.

"It can't be good for her digestion."

Wyatt didn't argue, not knowing much about cat digestion. "Anyway, to answer your question, no, we are not going to eat pizza and go to sleep. We are in fact going to eat pizza, then have sex again, then go to sleep."

"Oh."

Wyatt looked up at her and could see the small smile that played around her lips.

"Can I do that thing again with my mouth?" She was going to kill him. In the best possible way.

"Absolutely. Only if I get to do that thing with my mouth, too."

"Okay...I mean, if you insist."

That was his girl.

"Don't forget we still need to pick up my loaner car from the hospital. Plus my purse and everything is still in my locker. God, my locker. I remembered those pictures from yesterday. I should file charges against Logan. I can do that, can't I? For invading my privacy?"

"Abso-freakin'-lutely."

They had parked across the street from the police station. Camille was chattering to hide her nerves, but Wyatt didn't seem to mind. In fact he seemed to encourage any thoughts she had regarding taking action against Logan.

She came around the car and stopped. Suddenly crossing the street took on a whole new level of scary.

Wyatt held out his hand and she grabbed it.

"I haven't had to hold anyone's hand to cross the street in a long time."

"Yeah, well, you're holding mine from now on. We see a black car and we're getting back in the Jeep."

But there was no black car. In fact, early on a Monday morning, past normal morning rush hour there wasn't much traffic on the main street.

Together, they made it across. Once inside the police station they found an officer minding the main desk. Behind him, Camille could see that there were hardly any other officers milling about.

"We're looking for the sheriff," Wyatt said.

"He's working on a case."

He scowled. "Yeah, I can pretty much bet you this is bigger."

"I doubt it," the young man in uniform said.

"Look, can you tell us where to find him," Wyatt pleaded. "We need to update him on some new events that took place relating to the murders going on at Physicians' Memorial."

"Uh, he's at Physicians' right now."

Camille felt dread flood her system at the officer's words. Was he making an arrest? Had they found the proof they needed against Delia?

"Come on, Wyatt. We need to go."

Not arguing, he took her hand and they sprinted back to the Jeep. The trip to the hospital seemed like an eternity, but really Wyatt had gotten them there within minutes. Cop cars with lights flashing blocked the main entrance. It appeared people were being stopped before being let through the doors.

"This seems a bit much if they were going to arrest her."

Wyatt, too, looked puzzled. "Only one way to find out."

They approached the two officers who were checking identity and Wyatt stepped forward. "What's going on?"

"Sir, there is a crime scene in the hospital. I'm going to have to ask you what your business is in the hospital."

"I'm Dr. Holladay, this is Dr. Larson. We work here."

"You can go in. But please know the top floor will not be accessible."

Wyatt turned to her. "The administration floor."

The dread and sense of surrealism Camille had been feeling earlier doubled. This wasn't happening. Crimes happened in dark alleys in big cities. Not in small suburban America. Not in hospitals where people came to be healed.

"Wait." The other officer who had been checking ID stepped forward. "You said you're Dr. Larson? Dr. Camille Larson?"

"That's right."

"Sheriff Mooney is upstairs. He tried to contact Dr. Holladay this morning."

Wyatt immediately reached for his back pocket. "My cell. Damn it. I must have left it at the house."

"I'll call up and let him know you're on your way."

Camille knew her legs were moving forward. She knew

Wyatt was pushing the up button on the elevator. She knew she was heading some place she didn't want to go. Her brain wanted to rebel but her body kept moving forward.

"It's going to be awful," she whispered as the doors opened to the administration floor.

"Let's wait and see."

Yet another fresh-faced uniformed officer stopped them before they could proceed down the hallway. He pointed them to a series of chairs that had been set out against a wall, letting them know they couldn't move past that point.

Beyond the chairs was Ruby's desk. Beyond that Delia's office. Camille could see the activity inside. There were people inside talking. All kinds of movement. Someone taking pictures.

What could they be taking pictures of? What was happening behind that door? Camille felt an intense desire to leave before anyone could say anything and make it real.

"Oh, my God. Dr. Larson!"

The door to the ladies' room closed behind Ruby. Her face was a horrible color. As if her fake tan had been replaced by a fake sunburn. Her eyes were swollen and red, streaks of mascara ran down her face. Her teeth chattered and her hands shook as though she was freezing cold.

"Oh, it's so awful. It's so awful." She choked on her tears.

Camille moved toward her and patted her back in what she hoped was a comforting gesture. She angled her to one of the seats and encouraged her to sit. Fearing shock, she looked to Wyatt. "We're going to need a blanket."

He nodded and went in search of a linen closet.

"What happened?" Camille asked gently.

"I came in and found her like that. I was, like, 'Morning

Ms. Marsh.' That's what I say every morning. She's always in before me. She's, like, a workaholic. I'm always saying she shouldn't work as much. I'm always saying that."

The elevator dinged and Camille looked up to see Wyatt returning. He carried a thin hospital blanket and shrugged, knowing it wouldn't provide that much warmth. But anything would help. Camille wrapped it around the young girl's shoulders and used her hands to try and help her circulation.

"What did you see, Ruby?"

"Her," she said. "I saw her. She was hanging there. It was like something out of a horror movie. I kept waiting for her to lift her head up and be all, like, monster zombie or something like that. But she didn't move. She hung there. Her shoe fell off."

Sickened, Camille closed her eyes. She stood.

"Don't, Camille," Wyatt said. "You don't need to see that."

"I have to," she whispered, although she wasn't sure he heard. She had to know. She had to see what Delia had done.

The door was ajar. The people inside were still taking pictures, still having low conversations with each other. Before anyone could stop her, Camille pushed the office door and watched it swing open.

There, over the desk littered with papers the way it always was, Delia hung from the ceiling. Her face was swollen, her body still. Ruby was right, Camille thought, her shoe had fallen off.

Instantly the officers in the room reacted, pushing her away from the scene. Wyatt got there, too, turning her around, forcing her to look away, burying her face in his shoulder.

But it was too late. She'd already seen her.

"She's dead."

Wyatt didn't have to acknowledge that statement.

"Dr. Larson. Dr. Holladay."

Camille gulped the nausea in her throat. She looked at Wyatt and took a deep breath before turning around. "Sheriff."

Sheriff Mooney's face was grim. Lined with more than age, it was clear to her now that he'd seen too many things in the course of his life. Delia's body was one more.

"Let's have a seat." Deliberately he pulled the chairs away from where Ruby sat. The girl had her face in her hands and was rocking back and forth. One of the uniformed guards stood over her, a helpless expression on his face.

Wyatt took Camille's hand and the two of them faced the sheriff, waiting for his explanation.

"I'm sorry. It appears that sometime late last night Delia Marsh committed suicide."

Camille shook her head. "She wouldn't have done that. She wouldn't have done that before she heard about the grant money. I'm sure of it."

"Camille," Wyatt said gripping her hand.

"Of course," she muttered. "I'm being ridiculous. There she is, in that room, hanging there. I can't believe..."

"She left a note." The sheriff shifted his chair closer. "I can't show it to you. The crime scene specialists are in there now collecting evidence and taking prints. Once we have everything we need we'll take the body down. But I read the note. In it she claims responsibility for the deaths of Donald Morose, Samuel Ross and Janet Hamilton."

"No." Camille couldn't believe it. Even though it made sense. Even though she'd felt Delia's anger and... insanity, she didn't want to believe that a woman who had dedicated her life to building a hospital would destroy it with death.

"She says she was in love with Dr. Logan Dade. She discovered that he had feelings for you. Feelings that because they weren't reciprocated made him seek other employment. It was odd. In a way, she blamed you for not loving him and causing him to leave. As if you had control over what this other doctor did. She wanted to destroy you. Professionally."

"Not professionally," Wyatt interjected. "We came to the station this morning to report an attempt on Camille's life."

"Explain."

Wyatt did. He told the sheriff of their trip to see Dr. Dade in an attempt to get some answers, then the attack on them by the car with the tinted windshield.

Sheriff Mooney nodded. "It makes sense. She follows you, sees that you've gone to visit her ex-lover. Maybe she fears what he'll tell you. She snaps, tries to kill you, but when that fails she knows she's going to be found out. She'd already admitted to the vandalism. I was taking a hard look at her alibis for when the deaths in the hospital occurred. She was here for each one of them. I was getting close to bringing her in for questioning. She took her own life before that could happen."

"If you knew Delia…" Camille didn't finish the thought. It was silly to say that she wasn't the type. It was even sillier considering that she would have also said she wasn't the type to kill. Both things were now true.

"So it's over," Wyatt concluded.

"There are some loose ends to clean up. We still have to examine the body. We found something under the victim's nails we're going to need to analyze. Also, the note was typed, not handwritten. The prevailing thought with suicides is that the note should be personal, but a typed note isn't all that uncommon today given people's use of computers. Also, I'm going to want to find that black car you described. If we can find physical evidence of her in the car, then we'll be able to prove our assumptions. I'm sure all of us will rest better."

"No," Camille said quietly. "I won't. Not for a while."

"Understandable, Doctor. But you have to know none of this was your fault. You got caught in the middle between an unstable woman and her lover. It was bad luck on your part."

Bad luck. Three innocent lives lost. Another life gone. All for love. No, not even love. What Delia in her sick and twisted mind thought was love. What Logan in his strange and perverted ways thought was love.

There was no real love involved in any of this. For the first time she let herself think about what Wyatt had told her yesterday. He said it. The *L* word. She'd reacted so strongly she'd run from him. It wasn't in her nature to accept love. A perfectly logical premise given her history of abandonment by her parents.

Of course, her grandfather, the only one who cared enough to keep her, couldn't show or accept love or affection of any kind. He was a brilliant man in so many ways. And now she thought maybe he was right in this. Love was a word that got passed around a lot. A word people used when it was convenient, never realizing the pain that followed when someone left.

Camille had witnessed so-called love and none of it had been pretty. The love that Delia felt for Logan was destructive. Abusive. The love her grandfather had for her was controlling. And the love Wyatt thought Logan harbored for her, was sick and obsessive. That wasn't love.

Maybe her very controlled, very isolating world was the safest place for a person to be.

"Come on, Camille. I'm taking you home." Wyatt said to the sheriff, "We'll be around if you have any questions for us."

"Appreciate it."

The two men shook hands, then Wyatt helped Camille to stand.

"What about Ruby?" she asked, her gaze shifting to the young girl still rocking in the chair.

"We've called her parents. They're on their way to pick her up."

Knowing that was the best thing for her, Camille let Wyatt lead her to the elevators.

"I need to get my stuff. Out of the…locker." Camille had a hard time getting the word out. She didn't know if the cameras were still there. Most likely Logan dismantled them when he left, but it wouldn't matter. She would never change in that locker room again.

She'd have the next CEO see to it that she had her own office, her own private shower.

The next CEO. Not Delia.

Camille could feel the tears welling up, but she tamped them down. She didn't want to process everything that she had seen and heard until she was alone. Away from the eyes of the hospital. Nurses and doctors were milling about, talking, gossiping. By now everyone knew. They had to. What a scandal. Delia and Dr. Dade. Dr. Dade and Dr. Larson. Dr. Larson and Dr. Holladay.

Death. Murder. Love triangles.

Wyatt followed her into the locker room and stood by as she pulled out her purse. She found her keys and then he followed her to her car.

"I'll drive."

"I can drive."

"Camille, you've seen—"

"A dead body. Not my first. I can do this."

"Fine. But don't lose me. I'm following you all the way home."

Home. It was the second time he'd used that word. The second time he'd referred to his place as her home. It had felt like home. Last night in his arms. It had felt safe and protective.

Or was it him that made her feel like that? Like she was...loved.

Camille forced the word from her mind. She couldn't think about that now. She couldn't count on her feelings. She certainly couldn't count on his. Everything that had happened had been too much. She trusted none of it.

All she needed to do was go back to Wyatt's house. Aphrodite was there. She could collect her pet and then she would go to her home. The place that she had called her sanctuary, her safe haven, for so many years.

Her home didn't feel as good as being with him....

No. She couldn't let herself think that way. She wasn't going to fall into the trap of thinking that now that the danger had passed she could have her own happily-ever-after ending. Wasn't everything that had happened proof the fairy tale simply did not exist?

She glanced in the mirror. Wyatt was no more than a few feet from her bumper. Both hands were on the wheel of the Jeep, and his expression was intense, as if he could keep her close to him with the power of his mind.

The answer was so blindingly clear. Right now, in this moment, all she wanted to do was hit the accelerator. Speed away from him. Leave him in the dust. Get away from him because, deep down, she was more afraid of him than she was anyone else.

Foot on the pedal, she pressed down hard.

Chapter 16

"What the hell were you doing?"

Camille looked over her shoulder. As soon as she parked the car, she jumped out and made a dash for the house. Wyatt had shown her where the hidden key was and she used it to let herself in. She knew she only had minutes before he caught up to her. And the further along with her escape, the better.

Only he'd been very close behind her even after her attempt to elude him. It was going to make things harder.

"I'm packing."

"I asked you not to lose me," he said. "What was that stunt at the hospital?"

"I'm in a hurry."

"A hurry to do what? Will you stop that? I was hoping we could chill out for a while. Talk it all out."

"What is there to talk about? Delia is dead." Camille paused. The pain of it roared over her. She knew she shouldn't be this upset. The woman had wanted to kill her after all, but she couldn't get past the idea that a few days ago she thought Delia was the closest thing she had to a female friend. Now she was gone.

"That's it. She's dead. It's over."

"Isn't it? I know you brought me here because you wanted to protect me. That was very sweet of you. But the danger is past. I need to go home."

Camille was scooping up her clothes and throwing them into the overnight bag she'd brought with her. She tried not to look at him, but when she did she flinched in reaction to his expression. He did not look happy.

"*Sweet* of me. You think I did this to be *sweet*."

"I think you did this because you felt you had to."

"Bullshit. You know why I did this. You know why I brought you here that night after the break-in. You know why you slept in my arms last night. When are we finally going to talk about the fact that I told you I love you?"

The *L* word. There it was again, the one word she couldn't face. It made her afraid. It made her want to escape. She didn't take time to question why that was, she just accepted how she was feeling. Like a cornered rabbit.

Maybe if he hadn't used it, she could have stayed. Maybe she could have pretended that they were really close with nothing threatening happening between them. But he wouldn't let it go.

She zipped up the bag and slowly turned to face him. "I'm not sure what you want me to say."

"Uh…let's see…maybe that you love me, too."

Her body practically jolted. If she was frightened by the idea of him loving her, then she had no word for what it would mean for her to reciprocate his feelings. There was no name for a fear that big.

Love Wyatt? Love him. Give herself to him. Trust him with everything?

Haven't you already done that?

The sly voice inside her head was to be ignored. Now, more than at any other point in her life, she had to be reasonable and sound.

"I can't love you."

"*Can't*. There is that word again. You used it the first time I asked you to dinner. You said you couldn't date me."

"Exactly. I don't think a relationship between us would work. Therefore the logical step for both of us in order to avoid further pain would be to not pursue this…" Camille waved her hand between them rather than actually use the word *relationship*.

Wyatt stepped closer. "Am I hurting you?"

Yes! You're scaring me. You're making me believe I can have something I know I can't.

The words stuck in her throat. If she said them, he would try to counter her arguments. He was a good debater. He might win and then what would she do?

"I think we've kept things superficial enough to avoid any real pain."

His eyes narrowed. "Last night was superficial? That night we spent at your place…superficial?"

Camille tried to smile, but failed. "So typical of a man. You go right to sex."

"If my memory serves, you went right for my sex. And your mouth was about the least superficial thing I have ever felt in my life."

She could feel her cheeks heating. She hated that she was vulnerable to him on this level. "Sex is not love."

"Yes it is. When it's done the way we did it. You've never put your mouth on a man in your life, Camille. You think doing that with me meant nothing? You ever straddle a man before, ride him until you couldn't see straight? You ever let a man go down on you? Ever? You ever trust anyone that much?"

She backed away as he moved closer to her with each question. She found herself cornered against the bed in the guest room and in a fit of childishness, stepped onto the mattress and walked over it to avoid him. She escaped out the door leaving her overnight bag behind.

All she really needed was Aphrodite anyway.

"So you're going to run from this. Coward!"

Camille whipped around, her anger finally getting the better of her fear. "You don't understand."

"Make me understand. Make me see why we can't be together. I love you. I know, deep down in that messed-up heart of yours, that you love me, too. We can make this work."

"I can't! I can't trust. I can't give you anything. I don't know how. I've never known how. I want to be alone."

"Alone for the rest of your life. That's your solution."

"Yes! Look at what happened to Delia. She had her work and she was fine. Then she fell in love, tried to give herself to a man. And it drove her insane. That's what love did to her."

"You are not Delia," he said, his voice calmer.

"No. I'm worse. I have all these hang-ups. I didn't even make it through therapy. I can't stand to eat in a restaurant. I went crazy because I fell into some trash. You have to wash your car because I can't stand to touch anything that has the smallest amount of dirt on it. And I need a mask when I enter the clinic because all I see are the germs."

"So you've got hang-ups. You're a person, Camille. We

all have our thing. I can't drink. I can't take a sip of wine without wanting to drink the whole damn bottle. Why? Because I'm afraid I'm not good enough. I'm afraid I've never been good enough. So I like to sabotage myself any chance I get."

"There. You see? What if I'm that to you? What if I'm the next thing you're using to sabotage yourself with? I know," she said in a ridiculous voice. "I'll date crazy Dr. Larson. If I can succeed with her and her host of issues, I can make it with anyone."

"Stop that. It's not true and it's not fair to me or my feelings for you."

"I make no sense with you," she cried. "None. But you keep pushing me."

She reached for the door to the laundry room. Inside was Aphrodite's travel case. She picked it up and held it to her chest like a shield.

He stepped closer, his movements cautious as though she was the cat he wanted to trap.

"You're right. You don't make sense with the person I was. That person liked it easy. Easy life. Easy love. Easy marriage. All of it was easy. You are hard. You are like the Mount Everest of love. But I need you like I need sobriety. That's hard, too. But it's made me a better person. You make me a better man. It's so clear to me. And what upsets me is that the only thing preventing you from seeing it, too, is your damn insecurities."

"My damn insecurities stem from a lifetime of people leaving me. Why do I want to give you a chance to be the next in line? You say that I'm hard and that's what you need. But you won't say that a year from now. A year from now I'll still be hard, but you'll be tired of me. I know it."

"A year from now I'll only know you more. A year from

now I'll want to know you even more than that. Camille, I will never tire of you."

She shook her head. She couldn't believe him. There was nothing in her life that made having faith in him a sensible decision. "I need to go."

"Okay." He raised his hands and took a few steps back. "I've done this dance with you before. I get it. I come on a little strong—"

"You kept calling this place home," she accused him. "Like we lived here together. Like we were a family."

"I'm not going to lie. I want that for us. But I can wait. We can take it slow. We can go back to dating. I'll let you throw water in my face any time you want."

He was trying to make a joke. To lighten the mood. But it wasn't funny. That date, when she tried so hard to make it work, was nothing more than a symbol of her failure.

"I wish I was braver. I really do. But I'm not."

As if Aphrodite knew it was time to make a strategic exit she came right to Camille. A little persuasion and she had her locked in the travel case.

Wyatt hadn't responded to her last words. He stood in the living room with his hands in pockets. Not moving, head down.

But he didn't look defeated. He looked as if he was planning the next salvo. She needed to get out now, before he could fire it.

"I'll see you at the hospital," she said softly. She would do everything she could to avoid him. She would try not to speak to him for a while. But someday in the future, when he'd moved on, maybe they could go back to what they had been before all of this started. Acquaintances.

Wyatt listened to the sound of the door closing behind her and thought about shouting. Did real men shout? Not like a squeal or a crying shout. More like a caveman grunt that exclaimed to the world that his woman was causing him grief. That's what he wanted to do.

He threw himself down on the couch and thought about the look on her face when she left. He'd never seen anyone so frightened in his life. How did an intelligent woman fear so much what most of the world took for granted? He'd known she had issues, but he'd never truly understood how thick and heavy the wall around her heart was.

Because the two times he'd made love to her, there were no defenses. She'd been so open to him, so accepting. Had he mistaken those moments? Read into them more than there was?

Maybe she didn't love him. Maybe she liked having sex with him, but that was all she wanted.

That sucked.

He felt bereft and it was such a strange thing. There was no more action for him to take. Nothing he could use to stay in Camille's world. The events of the past week were abruptly over. She didn't need his protection. She didn't need any more favors from him. There would be no more bargains. And she wouldn't accept his love.

Hell, she wouldn't even accept a date.

Which left him…with failure.

Standing, he made his way to the kitchen. He opened the door of the refrigerator and found the nearly full bottle of white wine he'd bought for her. He'd coaxed a glass into her to calm her after the near-accident, but the bottle was still almost full.

He pulled it out and eyed it. He hadn't touched a drop in five years, so there was plenty left in this bottle to do the job. Drunk, he would stop thinking about her. Drunk, he would think only about staying drunk.

Booze made him forget. It had always worked that way.

The truth would creep up on him, want to take over, and a glass or two or three or four would drown it out. And he wouldn't have to listen to it until the next time.

So what was the truth? She didn't love him? She couldn't love him? Did it matter?

The result was the same. He was alone and the woman he couldn't seem to stop wanting was so far out of his reach that he was standing here looking at a bottle of wine.

Disgusted, Wyatt pulled the cork out and emptied the contents of it into the sink. He wanted to call her up and yell at her if only to tell her how much her stubbornness upset him. She'd almost driven him to drink.

Camille.

Staring around his now empty town house he thought about the next step. As a recovering alcoholic he'd always been about the steps. They made things simple, clear cut. Do one then the other.

Now he was on another precipice and it was time to figure out what came next. Step one: he could listen to her. Conclude, as she had, that she wasn't capable of a relationship because of the issues in her past. Step two: he could focus on his work, dedicate himself to the clinic until he forgot why having a life was important. Step three: he could start dating other women if work no longer became enough.

Step four: he could forget her. Or at the very least, he could push her far enough into his memories that she would be nothing more than a sad regret. A lost chance at something good.

It was a good plan. She would appreciate it. It was thoughtful, sensible and based entirely on the conclusion that she didn't return his feelings.

And he would be damned if he was going to follow through with it.

He'd called her Mount Everest for a reason. He imagined those who conquered that mountain did so after making a few attempts at it first.

Which meant he needed some new steps.

Step one: give her a night to think about it. Step two: she was going to need him at Delia's funeral. Camille would go, he knew that much about her. It didn't matter the circumstances around Delia's death, Camille would want to be there. Step three: hold her hand. Because that day, when it came, was going to suck for her, and any comfort he could give her he would.

Because he loved her.

Damn it.

Wyatt tossed the empty bottle into the recycling bin and cursed his luck for having to have picked the absolute most messed-up woman on the planet to love. Some things though, a man couldn't control. He was heading into the living room to strategize his new series of steps when his phone on the countertop caught his attention. He wasn't surprised that he'd forgotten it this morning, given his preoccupation with the events the night before. He was about to shove it in his pocket when he checked and saw that he had a new message.

Punching in his security code he listened for a second when the sound of a voice only vaguely familiar came through the speaker.

"Holladay, it's Dade."

That's why the voice was off. The broken nose he'd delivered had made Logan sound nasal. Wyatt's teeth clamped down at the recognition of who he was listening to as the pictures from the CD raced through his mind. He should have broken more than the jerk's nose. He should have ripped off his—

"Listen, I was thinking about what you said. Maybe I

feel a little guilty. I don't know. The thing with Camille...I couldn't get over her not wanting me. I figured that meant she was special. With a scalpel, she was better than I was. I can admit it. I don't like it, but whatever. Look, that's not why I'm calling. You asked if there was anyone I was worried about going off the deep end when I left. I know Delia was a problem, but she didn't worry me nearly as much as Jeff."

Jeff? Wyatt couldn't have heard that right.

"I told you I liked nurses. I liked all the nurses. I don't have any sex hang-ups. Men, women, it's all good to me. But Jeff sort of took things a little too seriously. He was convinced that in my heart I was gay and that we were meant to be together. I ended it with him. Let him know I liked to play it both ways. I even told him I was in love with Camille. That really set him off. He followed me for a while. I'm not going to lie. It made me nervous. It was either leave Physicians' Memorial or file a restraining order. Anyway, I thought you should know."

Wyatt listened to the message two more times, making sure he hadn't misheard. Logan Dade had hooked up with Jeff and Marie and Delia among others. But it was Delia who was responsible for the deaths. Wasn't she? Wasn't that what the note said—that Delia couldn't handle the idea that Logan didn't love her?

She snapped.

Wyatt understood that. Was he any better? Systematically plotting how he was going to get back into Camille's life? At least he was certain he wouldn't kill for her, or drive by her house waiting for—

A flash of memory clicked. He remembered when he'd gone to Camille's house to pick her up for the date that eventually ended in her bed. There had been a car parked across the street. He'd waited for the spot to open up.

A black car. A black car with tinted windows.

Had that been Delia? Had it been Delia who he chased through the woods that night Camille's house was broken into?

Wyatt picked up his cell and hit a button to dial his last received call.

"Hello?" Logan answered after a few rings.

"What kind of car does Jeff drive?" Wyatt asked without preamble.

There was a pause and Wyatt squeezed the phone in his hand as if it was the other man's neck.

"What kind of car does he drive?" he repeated slowly, his intent clear.

"Jeff is sort of a car nut. He likes old American cars. Has a bunch of them. One red, one black—"

"The black one. Are the windows tinted?"

"Yeah. He likes to mess around with guys in his car. Turns him on. He tints the windows so no one can see inside."

Wyatt hung up the phone, not needing to hear more. Delia hadn't done it. Delia hadn't tried to run them down on the streets of Philadelphia. Delia wasn't the murderer.

Delia was dead. Jeff wasn't.

And Camille was a sitting duck.

Chapter 17

Her cell phone wouldn't stop ringing. Given everything that had happened it wasn't as though Camille could ignore it. But when she saw the same name appear she tossed it into her purse.

"He's not giving up, Aphrodite."

Camille wished she could believe that her pet was offering moral support with her meow, but she knew the cat just wanted out of her cage.

Maybe Wyatt was going to turn out to be another Delia. What if he pursued her even against her wishes? As soon as Camille thought it, she knew it wouldn't be true. Wyatt was stubborn, but he wasn't a stalker. If she said no to him enough, eventually he would move on. Forget her. Put her firmly in his past.

Darn it.

Camille pulled up to her house and turned into the driveway. She ignored the insistent ringing of her phone and instead focused on getting an angry Aphrodite out of the car and into the house where she could release her.

She stopped when she saw Jeff get out of his car parked across the street. It was one of those cars that looked like it came out of a James Dean movie. Red, with racing stripes across the side.

"Dr. Larson," he said, jogging up to her. "I heard about Delia. I didn't know what to do. I couldn't believe it."

"I know." He took the carrier from her as she made her way to her front door. Part of her, the suspicious part of her that had developed over the last few days, wondered why he felt the need to come to her house. Her address wasn't a secret, but still, Jeff had never contacted her for any reason outside of work.

She opened the door and took Aphrodite from him.

"I guess I was curious what this meant for you... professionally?"

"I'm sorry?"

"Are you going to stay at Physicians' Memorial? I know it's probably crass to ask right now, but you're one of the best thoracic surgeons. It doesn't hurt my résumé working with you."

Okay, she thought. That was a somewhat legitimate premise for his being here. He wasn't concerned about Delia or her. He was concerned about his career. Only, he'd made that comment about Dr. Dade being a superior surgeon.

She glanced over his shoulder at the car he'd driven. The fact that the shape of it was similar to the black car that had nearly run her down made her nervous. But this car wasn't black, it was red. And Jeff was here to check about her future plans.

At least that's what her brain told her. Her gut was screaming something else entirely. She stepped inside and made sure there wasn't enough room for him to follow. She set Aphrodite down behind her and reached for the door.

"I really can't say what my plans are going to be now, Jeff. I need to let this all sink in."

"Of course. I understand. I felt like I had to ask you directly."

She nodded and smiled. That was all. He wanted to ask his question and see her reaction in person. It was plausible. She was merely unsettled by everything that had happened. Nothing wrong with that either.

"I can't see why I would leave," she offered. "Physicians' has been like a second home to me."

"That's good to hear."

With nothing left to say Camille began shutting the door. "Okay. Well, see you around the hospital."

His hand gripped the edge of the door hard, his foot blocking where she had tried to shut it. She felt the force of him shoving it hard against her. His strength sent her tumbling backward, tripping over Aphrodite's cage.

The cat let out a shriek. Or had Camille done that? All she knew was that it was over in seconds. She was on her butt and Jeff was inside the house, shutting and locking the door behind him. From the back of his shirt, he pulled out a length of rope.

"No."

He tilted his head to the side. "Sorry. I thought I could let it end with Delia. Let her take the blame for everything. Walk away from it all. But I couldn't let you live. Not now. When I had done all this because of you."

Camille tried to crawl away from him. Using her hands and heels like a crab she scooted back, but he had the advantage, towering over her as he followed her.

She flopped around so that she could gain her feet, but as

soon as she did, he grabbed her hair, pulling her up against his chest. His arm around her waist was like a vise.

"Stop this, Jeff. You're a nurse, you don't hurt people."

He laughed at that. "Doc, I signed up for nursing when I found out they were giving out huge signing bonuses. Plus I like hot doctors. They're all a little on the edge, if you know what I mean. They think they're larger than life, and sometimes they are. That's the only thing about nursing I care about. I don't give a shit about people. No, that's not true. I did care about one person. And he dumped me. Because of you."

She scrambled in his hold, trying to use her feet to kick at him, but her strength was only a fraction of his. He all but lifted and carried her into the living room.

Talking. She had to keep him talking. She needed time to think.

"I didn't—"

He grabbed her face in his hand, his fingers crushing her jaw as he turned her around. "I would beat you right now if I could. Beat you so bad that you looked on the outside like I've felt this past month. For a month I watched you, waited for that opening to hurt you and anything close to you. You don't know how badly I want to see you in pain. But I can't leave any nasty bruises. Except one place."

He grabbed her throat and squeezed. The air swooshed out of her. She clawed at the two hands around her neck, but couldn't budge him.

"Logan was mine. I knew, despite all the crap he pulled with the women in the hospital, that it was me he wanted. I knew it. But I couldn't get him to confess. He still had to hide that part of himself in the closet. I hated him for that! As much as I loved him, I hated that he wouldn't announce to the world that he was mine. That I was his."

Camille couldn't care less about where Jeff's anger came from as long as the time he was taking to tell her, was time he wasn't using to kill her. She could still breathe, but only barely. It was like he had complete control over how much pressure to exert to allow her enough air without crushing her larynx.

She thought about Marie and the sexual asphyxiation and knew instinctively where Logan had picked up such a trick.

"But no, he said he wouldn't be with me. He said he was in love. With *you*."

Camille could hear the outrage in his voice.

"You're nothing. You're this mouse with some weird talent for cutting into people. I told Logan he was better than you, told him how easy it would be to discredit you. Filling those syringes with air, sticking their IV hoses, it was so easy. They die, people stop thinking you invented open heart surgery, and Logan comes back. Only that didn't happen."

The lack of air was starting to affect her, she could feel her knees giving out. She dropped and for a second he let go of her throat. Instantly, she searched for something in reach. A candle jar on her coffee table. She grabbed it and swung it at him, hitting him in the face.

"You bitch!" he screeched as it bounced off his cheek.

Leaning down he picked her up by the wrist and threw her across the room into her bookcase. She felt her head smack hard against the edge and stars swam in front of her eyes.

"You're going to make this harder! The police need to believe you killed yourself. In a fit of guilt, unable to cope with the tragedy you brought on, you followed Delia's example."

"No one will believe that." Camille mumbled the words,

trying desperately to regain her thoughts. She needed a weapon. She had to act. She could see the rope that he planned to use, coiled in a loop on the floor around his feet.

"Delia said the same before I ended her, but the police will believe whatever you write. I really didn't want to kill her, but you had to go to the police. They were asking questions of all of us. No, I couldn't risk it. Someone had to be guilty and she was the most obvious suspect. With her dead, the police will stop looking. I'll make your letter especially good and then it will really be over. And once you're dead maybe finally Logan will see the truth. That you were nothing to him. Nothing to the hospital, to surgery. Nothing at all. He'll have to rethink everything, including our relationship."

Camille reached for and found the heaviest book on the shelf. *Gray's Anatomy.* She flung it at him, but it bounced off his chest. The power of her throw was nothing against the signs of mania he was exhibiting.

He reached for her again and she threw everything she had into a punch aimed at his nose. She'd seen how effectively Wyatt had subdued Logan with a single blow. But Jeff saw the move coming. He drew his face back and her fist glanced off the bridge, barely making contact.

Her attack only seemed to enrage him even more. She felt him grabbing her arm, taking both hands on it, one at her wrist and the other at her elbow. He brought it smashing down on the edge of the coffee table. She wasn't sure if it was the burst of pain or the sound of the bone cracking that got to her. She felt the edges of her sight go dark first.

Then everything went black.

Wyatt hung up the phone. It had been the hardest thing he'd ever done, but he knew the calmer he was in this scenario the better. He double-parked his car in front of the red one he knew belonged to Jeff.

At least that escape route would be cut off to him.

Wyatt focused on his breathing, even as he carefully and quietly approached the house.

Jeff was inside with Camille. Jeff was a murderer.

But Camille wouldn't be dead. She couldn't be.

For one, she'd barely left his place when he'd gotten the message from Logan. He'd chased after her, calling her cell the whole time. If only she had picked up the damn phone. But he couldn't worry about that now. He could only think in terms of time. He'd done eighty miles an hour through the small town without seeing a police car, although running into a cop on his way wouldn't have been the worst thing.

She could have only arrived at her house minutes ago. Jeff couldn't have killed her in minutes. You didn't take out a life, destroy a human being, in minutes.

The part of his brain that shouted to him that Jeff had done exactly that to those patients, he ignored. He needed to know she was alive. Believe she was alive. He made it to the front door. Carefully, he turned the knob and pushed to find it was locked.

The back door. Jeff had jimmied the lock during his break-in. It would be open, unsecured. Wyatt ran around the house to the rear. He climbed the porch steps and again turned the doorknob. This time it gave easily. Like a man attempting his own break-in, he opened it by degrees. Hearing each slight squeak, he prayed the noise wouldn't carry through the house.

He created only as much room as he needed to slide through. Once inside, he moved down the hallway on the balls of his feet, careful not to make any noise. He heard sounds coming from the living room. Heavy lifting. Pushes and grunts. Furniture shifting.

What he didn't hear was Camille fighting. What he didn't hear was Camille.

Lowering himself, he pressed his back against the wall ready to ease his head around the corner and take a look. If Jeff was looking in his direction, it was over and he would attack. If Jeff wasn't looking in his direction, he would attack and he would have the element of surprise on his side.

Not known for his fighting skills, Wyatt prayed he was up to taking the physically fit nurse down. Yesterday, he'd had no problem with Logan because he had rage on his side.

Today, he felt the same rage, but it was combined with desperation.

She isn't already dead. She isn't already dead.

It was the only thought he allowed himself to have.

In position he moved so that he could see into the living room. What he saw nearly stopped his heart. From the ceiling fan in the center of the room, Jeff had already hung the rope. He was holding Camille, who seemed to be unconscious, while he pushed her head through the loop at the end. The coffee table had been pulled over and now he set her standing on it so that the rope was slack. But the slightest nudge and she would fall.

She would hang.

For a brief second Wyatt allowed himself to think of Delia and what the end must have been like for her. He could only hope she, like Camille, had been unconscious when it happened.

With all the fury of a man seeing his woman in danger, Wyatt rushed at Jeff. He let out an awful shout and could see the noise startled the nurse who thought he was alone.

With his shoulder he knocked Jeff away, sending the man sprawling to the floor. Then instantly he reached for Camille. Jeff was nothing. Camille was everything. He grabbed her around the waist as she began to fall off the coffee table. The rope around her neck was holding her up but not strangling her.

"You fool," Jeff said as he got to his feet. "I'm going to have to kill you both."

With that the front door burst open. Two officers rushed in first, two others behind them.

Wyatt didn't blink at their arrival. The hardest, but the smartest, thing he'd done was call the police as soon as he spotted the red car out in front of Camille's house. His first instinct had been to rush to her rescue, but his second was that he needed backup.

"On the floor! Now!"

They might not have been city-trained cops, but the four officers who had burst through the door, guns pointed, seemed threatening enough to Wyatt.

To Jeff, too, apparently. After the briefest hesitation, he got down on the floor, arms spread.

"Camille, honey. You with me?"

Now that Jeff was secured, Wyatt dared to look up. Her eyes were closed but her coloring was fine. With one arm still wrapped around her waist, he lifted her so that he could work the rope off her neck. She flopped forward onto his shoulder and his heart kicked into overtime.

Carefully, he laid her out on the rug. The police were handcuffing Jeff, pulling him to his feet, and shoving him out the front door.

"Ambulance is on its way." Sheriff Mooney stood over him, an expression of concern etched in his face.

An ambulance. Wyatt didn't need an ambulance. He was

a doctor. He would fix her. Checking her pulse, he closed his eyes with relief as he found it strong and steady if a bit fast. Doing a quick assessment, he could see that her arm was broken. He moved it away from her body and the slight jostling must have sent a bolt of pain through her.

She groaned and the sound pierced his heart, but her eyes fluttered and he thought the pain was worth it if she would wake up.

"That's it, babe, wake up. Let me see those eyes. Tell me you're with me."

They opened, and he could see the glassy look of fear and pain in them.

"Jeff. Get out. Save—"

"They got him. The police have him. It's all over now. Really over."

"Arm," she mumbled.

Wyatt nodded. "Yeah. It's broken."

"Can't operate."

"No," he said. He waited for what would come next. Waited for the agony she would feel, not from the pain in her arm, but from the knowledge that for a time she wouldn't get to be the only thing she thought she was.

But instead of tears or heart-wrenching moans, she lifted her good hand to his face. He pressed his hand against hers, holding it in place, thinking how much he loved her touch. Any touch. Like there was magic in her skin.

"I almost lost you," he muttered, trying to keep his voice from cracking.

"No, you saved me. Wyatt?"

"Yes? What? Anything. The ambulance is on its way. Any second. We'll get you to the hospital. Get the arm set. I'll call in the best orthopedic, I promise."

"Ambulance. Make sure the stretcher…it's clean."

He nodded, and then he laughed, feeling the joy bubble

out of him. She was going to be all right. If she was worried about the stretcher being clean, then his Camille was going to be just fine.

Chapter 18

She opened the door to the establishment and paused, searching for her target. She spotted him in the back at a corner table. He was reading the paper and didn't see her at all.

Camille took a moment to look around at the people drinking coffee and eating scones and muffins. She inhaled the smell and thought that it didn't bother her as much as it used to. The countertop where people sat on stools resting their elbows didn't look like the germ fest she used to think it was. The tables where others sat appeared to shine with polish.

The mugs in their hands were gleaming white.

Still, Camille had brought her own personalized coffee mug with her. There were some limitations after all.

She made her way to Wyatt's table and cleared her throat as a way of announcing her presence. The paper in his hand crumpled as he peered over it.

"Hi."

He waited a beat. "Hi."

"Can I sit?"

"Sure."

Okay, so she knew it wasn't necessarily going to be easy. Eating crow never was.

And she deserved to suffer a bit in this moment. Wyatt had been a rock for her while she was in the hospital. He'd saved her life and sat with her through the recovery. He'd held her unbroken hand during Delia's memorial service.

All the while, she had been less than an appreciative patient.

The damage hadn't been light. Jeff had broken her tibia clean through. A team of the top orthopedic surgeons in the country had been called in for the consultation and it was decided that surgery as well as pins to hold the bone in place were required.

Wyatt's had been the last face she saw before going into the O.R. and his was the first face she saw when she came out. He was there for her for the subsequent days while they waited to see if any nerve damage had been done.

There wasn't.

However, once the arm was in a cast and she was free to leave the hospital, she wanted to go home. Her home. He didn't fight her. He didn't insist she stay with him or force his presence on her. She could see the fight they had before Jeff's attack was still in the air between them. And she knew that he had resigned himself to let her figure a few things out on her own.

She'd done an excellent job of convincing him that she didn't need him.

Darn it.

He drove her home from the hospital, assured her that Aphrodite had been well cared for during her hospital stay and promised that he would be there if she needed him. Then he kissed her on the cheek and said goodbye.

For a moment, sitting in that car with him in front of her house, she'd been tempted to invite him in. To ask him to stay with her because she didn't want to be alone. Not for a day. Or for a week. But forever.

It wasn't fair. She knew that instinct was based on the lingering fear she felt from Jeff's attack and her new fear of what the future might hold if her arm didn't heal properly.

He deserved better than fear. So did she.

If she was going to ask him to stay, it had to be for the right reasons. Which meant she needed to work through a few of her issues first. The most prevalent being how she was going to handle not being a surgeon for the foreseeable future. The cast would be on for eight weeks. Therapy would take weeks after that to regain her strength. The day-to-day future, which had been so set in stone for a bulk of her life, had suddenly shifted.

What if she wasn't the surgeon she was before? What if surgery of all kinds was out of the question?

What if she was just Camille Larson?

She had needed days to overcome that. In truth, a good two weeks had passed before she had finally begun to stir from the catatonic paralysis she'd fallen into after being released.

But after those weeks alone, after coming to grips with the death of her patients, making the calls of condolences to their families and mourning Delia, she'd been left with the reality that she hadn't evaporated from existence.

Weeks of not operating on anyone and she didn't fade away into the stratosphere. She didn't become invisible. She didn't want to throw herself off a bridge or commit herself to a nunnery.

She lived. She breathed. She functioned.

It was during that time when she couldn't face the hospital, Wyatt or any of the things that happened to her in the weeks before the attack that she began to take walks. She began to breathe fresh air and watch as people went about their days, living their lives. People who could hold hands. Couples who kissed each other in public. Mothers who wiped the runny noses of their children.

People who were connected to other people.

Camille decided it was time to try new things. Theaters that had been taboo could be conquered with a discreetly purchased plastic cover that fit over the seat. Restaurants weren't nearly as scary as long as she inspected the glasses and the plates carefully. Gyms...well, they were still completely too sweaty for her to attempt, but she had tried.

After all, she'd been dumped into a trash bin and survived that. Was anything else as awful? She'd almost been killed. Didn't that mean she could live through anything? She was beginning to think so. Beginning to believe.

So she sat across from Wyatt and when the girl serving the tables came over, Camille pulled her mug from her purse and removed the plastic wrap. "I'll have whatever he's having."

"Right," the waitress said.

"Can you ask them...not to touch the rim of the mug too much?" After all, she was still a work in progress.

"Gotcha." The girl left with the mug and Camille tried to avoid Wyatt's intense scrutiny.

"You know that stuff will kill you."

"Everything in moderation is acceptable." She hoped.

"You brought your own mug?"

"A compromise. I decided that I couldn't avoid eating or drinking establishments forever. I can't bring my own utensils and plates to a restaurant without looking weird, but here it's perfectly acceptable to carry a personal mug. So I do."

He smiled and folded the paper in half, and then again as if he was done reading it.

"What brings you here?"

"Several things."

"This," he said with a smirk as he leaned back in his chair, "ought to be good. Proceed."

"I don't know that I properly thanked you. For saving my life...twice. For being there for me in the hospital, for taking care of Aphrodite—"

"Next," he said in a flat tone. "This bores me. I don't want or need your gratitude."

There was a reason they called it crow, she thought. The feathers were sticking in her throat. "I wanted to let you know that I've taken some time to think about things."

He moved toward her then, his elbows now resting on the table. "Go on."

"I had to come to grips with the fact that I couldn't be who I had been trained to be. At least for a few months. The cast is off." She raised her right hand.

"I noticed."

Of course he did. "But I still need several weeks of therapy to regain full mobilization. And then I need to go back and do cadaver surgery. After that I'll need to assess where I am physically. No doubt I'll need to be reviewed and perhaps overseen during surgery at least for the foreseeable future until everyone is convinced I'm back to normal."

"You'll get there."

"Normal?"

"No, not there. You'll get back to being the surgeon you were."

"How can you be so confident?"

"Because I know you. I know how hard you'll work. According to the docs—and I've consulted many—there should be no permanent damage and if that's the case, you won't let anything like time or pain or people watching over your shoulder stop you. You'll do what has to be done to be the best. Not because you need to be, but because your patients need you to be. You'll do it for them."

He was right. And she let herself smile because, despite everything that had happened between them, he knew her so well and he never tried to hide that.

"I think you're right. But in this time of waiting I've had a chance to reevaluate myself."

"Go on."

"I've been able to recognize that some of my fears are unfounded. My neuroses, while based in childhood trauma, are not insurmountable with some determination and hard work."

"Have you been back to see Dr. Rosen?"

"No. I've been practicing."

"Uh-oh."

"I've been going to restaurants."

"Oh, my."

"I've been trying not to sanitize my silverware before eating, but I usually cave."

"Amazing progress. Why?"

"Because if a person is going to date someone," Camille gulped. "Well, she has to learn how to eat out, and drink coffee at coffee shops and have a glass of wine at the bar. That's what couples do."

He smiled. "And have you been practicing dating?"

She sighed, sensing that at this point he was teasing her more than testing her. "I have not. I discovered that I don't care for the idea of dating lots of different people.

Truthfully, there's only one person I imagine seeing myself with."

He crossed his arms over his chest and stroked his chin with his hand as if deep in thought. "I'm going to guess that's not Dr. Logan Dade."

She smiled. "You would be correct."

"So who is this mysterious person with whom you wish to practice date?"

Camille rolled her eyes. It wasn't as if she didn't know he would gloat. "I think I would like that person to be you."

"Why?"

Here, she decided. Now. It was time for the truth. "Because the one thing I learned through all of this is that I missed something more than being a surgeon."

"Really," he drawled.

She pursed her lips and glared at him. "You're not really going to make me say it."

"You bet your ass I am. Tell me, Camille. What could you have possibly missed more than surgery?"

"You." It wasn't as hard to say as she thought it might be.

His face took on an expression that she didn't know if she had ever seen before. Maybe he looked a little like her grandfather when she graduated from med school. But this was bigger than that. This was better. She was prepared to say that she loved him. She'd been practicing it for weeks. The words still stuck in her lungs, her throat, her tongue and sometimes her teeth. But if she worked really hard and took several deep breaths before trying, she could say it.

I love you, Wyatt.

But he nodded. "I have a better suggestion."

"I'm all ears."

"Practice dating can be stressful."

"Tell me about it." Camille pulled her blouse from her neck, feeling that it had grown damp from her sweat.

"You need a comfortable and safe environment."

"If you say so. I'm pretty much ready to agree to anything."

This time his smile was more than joyful, different than rueful. It was predatory and it made the hair on the back of her neck stand up in a good way. "I think if we were married you would feel more comfortable to explore yourself."

"Really," she drawled in a weak imitation of him.

"Yes," he said, standing only to come around the table and kneel before her. "I think if we were married, you could practice anything you wanted with no worries about failing."

"That might be a very conducive environment," she agreed. It was as though the hang-ups, the apprehensions, and the past…fell off her shoulders and onto the floor. She was a new woman…because of him.

"Marry me, Camille. For your own good."

She smiled and reached out to grab his hands, squeezing them. "I have always believed in taking the advice of a good doctor."

* * * * *

COMING NEXT MONTH

Available March 29, 2011

ROMANTIC SUSPENSE

SRSCNM0311

REQUEST YOUR FREE BOOKS!

2 FREE NOVELS PLUS 2 FREE GIFTS!

Silhouette®

ROMANTIC SUSPENSE

Sparked by Danger, Fueled by Passion.

ROMANTIC
SUSPENSE

Sparked by Danger, Fueled by Passion

SAME GREAT STORIES AND AUTHORS!

Starting April 2011,
Silhouette Romantic Suspense will
become Harlequin Romantic Suspense,
but rest assured that this series will
continue to be the ultimate destination
for sweeping romance and heart-racing
suspense with the same great authors
you've come to know and love!

*Selene wanted nothing to do with the father of her son,
Alex; but Aristedes had other plans…that included them.*

*Read on for an sneak peek from
THE SARANTOS SECRET BABY by Olivia Gates,
available April 2011, only from Harlequin Desire.*

"You were right to turn my marriage offer down," Aristedes said.

And Selene found her voice at last, found the words that
would not betray the blow he'd dealt her. "Thanks for letting me know. You didn't have to come all the way here,
though. You could have just let it go. I left yesterday with
the understanding that this case is closed."

Before the hot needles behind her eyes could dissolve
into an unforgivable display of stupidity and weakness, she
began to close the door.

The door stopped against an immovable object. His flat palm.

"I can't accept that." His voice was low, leashed.

What did her tormentor mean now? Was he ending one
game only to start another?

She raised eyes as bruised as her self-respect to his,
found nothing there but solemnity and determination.

Before she could voice her confusion, he elaborated. "I
never let anything go unless I'm certain it's unworkable. I
realize I made you an unworkable offer, and that's why I'm
withdrawing it. I'm here to offer something else. A workability study."

She leaned against the door, thankful for its support and
partial shield. "Your son and I are not a business venture
you can test for feasibility."

His gaze grew deeper, made her feel as if he was trying
to delve into her mind, take control of it. "It's actually the

SDEXP0411

other way around. I'm the one who would be tested."

She shook her head. "Why bother? I know—and *you* know—you're not workable. Not with me."

His spectacular eyebrows lowered over eyes she felt were emitting silver hypnosis. "You're right again. Neither you nor I have any reason to believe that isn't the truth. The only truth. It might be best for both you and Alex to never hear from me again, to forget I exist. But then again, maybe not. I'm only asking for the chance for both of us to find out for certain. You believe I'm unworkable in any personal relationship. I've lived my life based on that belief about myself. I never really had reason to question it. But I have one now. In fact, I have two."

Find out what happens in
THE SARANTOS SECRET BABY by Olivia Gates,
available April 2011, only from Harlequin Desire.

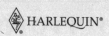

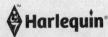